Pieces of Blue

by

Melanie Jackson

MW01534400

This book is a work of fiction. Names, characters, places and incidents either are products of the author's imagination or are used fictitiously. Any resemblance to actual events or locals or persons, living or dead, is entirely coincidental.

Copyright © 2012 by Melanie Jackson

Version 1.1 – August, 2012

All rights reserved, including the right of reproduction in whole or in part in any form.

Discover other titles by Melanie Jackson at
www.melaniejackson.com

ISBN 978-1479104338

Printed in the United States of America

Prologue

My eyes opened, looking for danger before my conscious mind knew I was alarmed. There was a moment of disorientation before I realized that I was in my great-grandfather's colonial bed with only the light from my watch and the wind for company.

The fire I had lit before bed had burned down, leaving only the faint smell of soot. The moon was near full, but still obscured by clouds so there was no more than a faint glow to show me where the windows were.

I listened. I looked at the shades of black. Nothing was there. Nothing at all. Whatever I had thought I heard or felt, it wasn't real.

A flash at the corner of my eye. I rolled my head. Light on the window—strobing, distant. The lighthouse of Goose Haven, I realized. Could that be what had awakened me?

I got out of bed. I didn't tiptoe but I walked softly. My socks were still on and they helped muffle my steps when I left the rug beside the bed. Down the stairs I went, cellphone in one hand and lamp in the other. I walked to one side of the steps, hoping it would minimize creaking. No one was there, of course. But still I wanted to be silent.

Step. Listen. Step. Listen. I stopped on the landing and held my breath. But there wasn't the smallest sound beyond the wind razoring through the garden and the last violent spatters of rain at the uncurtained window and the thudding of my heart. The house and I held our breath and shuddered at the brief assault, but nothing else happened.

Ghosts, I thought again, but banished the word immediately. I was ashamed it even crossed my mind, and the violence with which I rejected the possibility showed me how frightened I really was.

Down the steps I went on tiptoe until I reached the bottom. Then I smelled it. Felt it. Saw it in the lamp's brief, wavering light. Fresh air, a small drought creeping over the floor and then up my body as it encountered the obstacle of my legs and decided to explore my trembling body.

It was coming from the kitchen.

My eyes finally opened and I wondered groggily why I had been dreaming of my first night in Wendover House and what had woken me.

Nature answered with a violent flash of light which left a steady, luminescent glow in my window that was obvious even in the rain.

Which had not been predicted. We were supposed to be enjoying clear skies all week.

"What the devil is that? Kelvin?" I whispered, looking for my cat. As expected, he was gone. Barney whined from the depths of his doggie bed. He didn't like thunder.

Sighing, I got to my feet and went to the window to see how bad the storm was and what was causing the weird greenish glow. The storm was strong and heavy with rain, though the wind wasn't all that forceful. Perhaps my heavy-headed hydrangeas would survive.

There was indeed a strange grayish-green glow coming from the beach, which was bright even though it was raining like something from the Old Testament.

"What do you think?"

Storms in the islands mean something—and not just that the weatherman has goofed again. Storms are omens and harbingers. On an island, evil and good fortune both arrive by sea. I pay special attention to bad weather. It rarely brings the kind of messages that come with candy and flowers.

It seemed an appropriate moment, so I said a quick prayer of thanks that the house now had electricity. The situation was uncanny enough without creeping around by candlelight.

I didn't dress, but the bathrobe was ignored in favor of a raincoat. Slippers were traded for rain boots. Armed with a flashlight, I headed for the bedroom door. Barney galloped after me, less as a gallant protector than as one seeking protection.

"Kelvin!" I called and was not surprised to hear a meow coming from the front door.

The house is old, its doors and windows heavy. The hinges didn't shriek as I pulled the door open, but it felt like they should have.

Barney doesn't like storms but when Kelvin darted out, Barney followed. The one with the flashlight and bad eyesight brought up the rear.

Rot and ozone. *The smell of damnation.*

I'm agnostic about a lot of things but have always believed in statistics. The average freak factor for the "impossible" on the island was ten for ten. Something was happening down on the beach.

I had hoped to see a light at either of the two cottages below, indicating that someone else was awake. Ben or even Mary would be very welcome just then. But both houses were dark, so the three of us were left to make our way to the beach.

The glow began to fade just as I passed Ben's cottage. It was hardly evident when I finally reached the stony beach. All that was left to mark the spot was a small chest—about the size of a large jewelry box—encrusted with barnacles. And as I knelt, the unseasonably cold water drumming on my head in a painful manner, the last of the green light died.

The box was filthy and I didn't want to touch it. Because it was filthy. And because I just didn't want to touch it.

But if I left it to fetch some rags to wrap it in, would the tide haul it away again?

As I said, storms in the islands mean something. They are harbingers and omens. Ignore them at your peril.

Muttering under my breath, I pulled off my coat and wrapped the box in it. I had to wrestle with the strange seaweed trailing out of the surf that clung to it like a stubborn octopus. By the time it was free, my nightgown was giving a great impression of being my second skin, huddling as close as it could to my shivering body as the rain attacked it.

"Come on, guys," I said, turning to go back up the hill. "I'm getting soaked here."

As though only just noticing his wet fur, Kelvin streaked for the house. Barney doesn't streak so he trotted beside me as I jogged up the trail to the shelter of the family home. In my arms, the box felt warm and smelled unpleasantly of dead things.

"What the hell are you?" I asked it.

Chapter 1

I prospered in love and found the perfect wyfe. Tales of the family and island are queer and abundant, but the protection they offer suits. And she is a comely woman for all her strangeness and styll young enough to bear children yet so it may be that I shall have a son.
—from the unbound journal of *Halfbeard*

To stave off feelings of uselessness, I had started writing a blog that spring about island life—wildlife, regional stories, seafaring songs, and legends. It was unedited by a third party so people were getting me without any grammatical intervention. A couple of historical groups had picked me up anyway and I had gained a nice following of loyal readers. Voluntary donations weren't making me rich but they paid for blueberry pie and coffee. Once in a while someone would contact me about writing a freelance piece for some online magazine or periodical. Things were working out.

Except I hadn't written a word all that week.

It was to be hoped that when the encrustations were scraped away there would be something interesting underneath the living muck—a cache of ammunition from a warship, a map box, maybe some kind of top secret dispatch left over from the war. Or a ... an anything that I could turn into a story because I was running on creative fumes and coffee, and the java had just given out and the ferry didn't come until Tuesday.

It wasn't that there were no more stories to tell about Little Goose, but good taste and a continuing desire for privacy for myself and my neighbors had kept me from delving too deeply into my family's private experiences, especially the occult ones, though they were by far the most colorful, even lurid, subject I could imagine. However, telling their stories would bring out the kooks—the paranormal investigators and treasure hunters. Worse, any talk about a sea monster could bring marine biologists, legitimate scientists that could attract legitimate and popular media. So I was down to migrating puffins and porpoises and cranberry bogs, none of which interested me particularly.

A smart woman wouldn't have brought the box home. Except.... Well, I just couldn't have left it behind. It could have *anything* in it and who could resist such a mystery? Still, I didn't want to touch the box myself. It was somehow sinister and personally threatening. Even if it had arrived on a silver salver carried by a butler straight off the Queen Mary, I wouldn't have liked it. Fortunately other people aren't as squeamish.

As soon as it was a decent hour I would call my neighbor, Ben Livingston. He was a thriller writer and this sort of thing was his meat and potatoes. He would probably be enthusiastic about scraping the disgusting barnacles off the box and seeing what was inside. Ben wasn't plagued by intuition.

To entertain myself while I waited, I got out my digital camera and took some pictures of the box. To add drama I propped a damask pillow up behind the box where it sat dripping on the kitchen counter.

6:02.

Finally I went back to the library and pretended to dust the bookshelves.

The hands of the library clock finally worked themselves around to the seven and I felt that I could finally summon my neighbor who was usually an early riser. Barney and Kelvin had finished breakfast and were having a nap—I fear that Kelvin's sleeping habits have rubbed off on the dog—but Kelvin's ears twitched when I picked up the phone, telling me that he was at least in part still tuned in to the waking world.

"Hi, Ben."

"Good morning. Quite a storm last night." His voice was scratchy with disuse, but he seemed alert and not freaked out by seeing weird lights.

People in the islands have embraced a sort of fatalism about the unpredictable weather even when it conflicts with other, more widely held ideologies of science and reason. Stuff just happens here.

Or maybe he had slept through the greenish glowing stuff.

"Yes, it was. And it washed up something strange on the beach."

7

"Not a body, I trust." He wasn't joking. There had been a body last January.

"Nope. Some kind of small chest all crusted over with barnacles and things. I thought, since it could be Davy Jones' locker or something, that maybe you would want to be here when I open it." That was supposed to be a joke but I knew the moment the words left my mouth that Ben wouldn't take it that way.

"Absolutely. I'm on my wa—" The line went dead before he finished speaking. No time to ask him to bring coffee.

I stared at my phone for a moment and then turned it off. I was hoping that he didn't really expect Davy Jones' locker.

Since I had no more coffee, I went to make some tea. Fortunately, I had some scones from the day before. One needed to feed the help as they labored or they sometimes stopped and went away.

Ben arrived before the water boiled or even got properly hot. His presence woke Kelvin and Barney. Kelvin was mostly indifferent to his arrival but Barney was excited to see him.

"Where is it?" Ben asked, barely stopping to pet Barney, which left my dog baffled. What could be more important than petting him?

"In the kitchen."

Ben didn't wait for me to finish but strode toward the back of the house. He was breathing hard but that might be because he had run uphill. The island is a sort of tilted slab and the houses built like the old-style motte and bailey—with my house being the motte and the ocean being the really big moat that protected us.

Ben took the slimy box over to the sink, and ignoring the rubber gloves and more forceful of the tools I had laid out for him, began using a putty knife on the bulging corner. Handling the small chest did not seem to bother him. I found it to be repellant. It was filthy, leaking black ichor, and unnaturally warm. My stained coat was soaking in the bathtub. If it didn't come clean I planned to throw it away. I might throw it out anyway. It felt contaminated with some kind of psychic miasma.

"So what do you think it is?" I asked him. "A map box? A gun locker?"

8

Ben's grunt could indicate anything, but after a moment of silence he looked up briefly. His eyes were shining and I began to feel trepidation. Ben gets excited about things that are almost always troublesome for me.

"I've been doing some research on your seafaring ancestors and I have some pretty high hopes," he said. I knew he had been heavily involved in research the last month or so, but not that it involved my family.

"Yeah?"

"I've been looking at both Abercrombie, who died when the *Terminar* went down, and his son-in-law, Nicholas Robert Wendover. I haven't got definitive proof yet, but I believe Nicholas was really Robert Johnson, a.k.a. Robert Halfbeard, so called because an accident with some gunpowder left him unable to grow hair on half his face. He was wanted for robbery and criminal violence on the sea for the short time he sailed with Black Bart's flotilla. I think he was guilty of other crimes as well."

If the man had been a pirate, that went without saying. The idea was not a new one. Harris had mentioned a brigand in the family on our first visit to the island.

"That must have been a unique look." I didn't ask about Black Bart. I knew the story would be forthcoming if the box didn't open quickly. Ben liked to lecture and stories grew rapidly when they took root in the midden of Ben's devious mind.

"He abandoned his remaining facial hair almost immediately but the name stuck," Ben answered, putting down the knife, which hadn't been of much use, and picking up an upholstery hammer began tapping the shells away with more patience than I had imagined him capable of showing. "I haven't found out much about his early life, but his ship, the *Calmare*, came to a bad end right after he gave up his captaincy."

"What happened?" I pulled the plate of scones closer to me and tried to remember where the first aid box was. Ben was already dripping blood from his knuckles and fingertips. So far none had gotten on the box but I was afraid it eventually would. That seemed like a bad thing, though the chances of this box actually belonging to someone on the ship seemed slim.

9

"The ship went down in rough water with all hands aboard just off the Massachusetts coast. There were no known survivors and no wreckage was ever found. She wasn't huge, a single-masted sloop with fourteen guns, but she wasn't a small fishing boat either. There should have been some sign of her if the ship was destroyed."

I shivered.

"If there were no survivors then how do we know the waters were rough? Or that it even sank?" I asked.

"The captain of the *Acabar* logged seeing the *Calmare* the day previously so we know she was in the general area. Captain Darby—the former first mate—had stated to Nicholas Johnson when they laid on supplies his intention to sail for Boston on September ninth, so there is little chance that they were too far off the coast. They never made it to Boston—and records for other ships and those on land do not mention any storms except off the coast where New Hampshire butts up against Massachusetts. Sometime either on the night of the ninth or the morning of the tenth, the ship disappeared and was never seen again."

"Hm. Okay. I guess I'll swallow that. Could it have been an accident or sabotage? Some drunken cook or an insane crewmember who was flogged once too often and set the thing on fire out of revenge?"

"Maybe, but no one on shore saw a fire and they should have, even with rain. I mean, it would have been one hell of a bonfire and pretty close to shore. But no one saw a thing."

"So what do you think happened?"

"I don't think it was sabotage and of course they didn't deliberately fire the ship with everyone still aboard. If they were still aboard," he added to himself. "And they must have been. There are no records of the crew being seen again."

"So what then?"

"There aren't a lot of accounts outside of legal documents accusing Halfbeard of piracy, of course, but Halfbeard seems to have been a decent captain if a reprehensible human being. Very egalitarian and fair with splitting up the shares. Not particularly fond of the lash. He let the men drink. He also lacked imagination so unlike a lot of his contemporaries, he was not frightened by tall tales of sea monsters and ghost ships. It kept the crew calm."

"And so?" I wondered if he would ever get to the point and then asked myself if I really wanted him to. Sometimes, when I dine on the wrong kind of information, it gives me indigestion in the form of nightmares.

"Darby was another matter. He tended to drink and when inebriated, he claimed to have *the sight*."

"How stupid of him to admit it, if it was true. And even if it wasn't. Sailors were a superstitious lot." Even I knew this much.

"And by that point they already had reason to be fearful."

One by one the barnacles were surrendering their hold. I hoped that Ben would be willing to take them out to the back garden and throw them over the wall. I was sure that they were unwholesome.

"Now we're getting somewhere," Ben said with satisfaction. The box was wood, plain with iron hasps that had not rusted. The wood would indicate that the box was old, but the lack of rust was disappointing. If the hinges were stainless steel then it was modern.

"Why were they frightened? Beyond the obvious dangers of drowning, hanging, and fatal diseases?"

"Why indeed. Well, here the story gets wild. You have to keep an open mind."

"I'm open." Boy, was I! Ben had no idea. Little by little I had been alienated from my earlier beliefs and concepts about how the world worked. I still wanted natural, rational explanations for the strange things that happened around me, but was coming to accept that usually none would be forthcoming. At least none that could be shared with the outside world. "And I heard that wild is great for selling books."

"It's good for me, yes. Others around here may not like it."

That didn't sound good.

"Lay it on me anyway."

And he did. Ben began unpacking his mental suitcase of carefully researched information, laying out facts and inferred conclusions in a clear and attractive order. As a writer, I could appreciate his technique. As the holder of the creepy box I was less than thrilled with what he was saying. I could hear my grandmother saying, *no matter how you slice it, it's still just bologna.* But I couldn't dismiss it as nonsense, as much as I would have liked to, because of how the box had arrived.

"Rumor has it that the *Calmare* attacked the Spanish ship, *Concepcion.* Halfbeard did it for the cargo, but also because of race hate. He was very anti-Catholic." When I stared at him, he added, "Remember that the Reformation rocked Europe back on its religious heels, and the ongoing holy hatred followed the sailors into the New World and lingered there long after treaties were signed by the inbred kings and popes back in the old one. Halfbeard would have believed that killing Catholic Spaniards was practically his duty."

I nodded.

"The document trail is scanty but fairly clear in spite of the missing pieces. Halfbeard began following the *Concepcion* outside Hispaniola. Other ships saw him but kept back. He had a bad reputation. He'd been resting up in Tortuga de Mar when he saw her sail past and recalled the crew. A cabin boy was left behind and that's how we know where he was. *Concepcion* wasn't a large ship, but she was headed for Spain, which meant she had gold, and she was an enemy so he decided to attack her as soon as she was away from possible aid."

"What did he get for his troubles?"

"There is no surviving manifest of what the *Concepcion* carried, but there were rumors in Mexico of a cursed treasure."

I felt my eyes get big.

"A cursed treasure?"

"Yes. Mind you, according to legend a lot of treasures were cursed and that never stopped anyone from attacking ships. Maybe it kept the slaves from stealing things. Anyhow, Halfbeard didn't know about the curse and probably wouldn't have cared if he did. As I said, he was unimaginative. Showing both cunning and patience, he waited until the Spanish ship reached Florida and then continued sailing into the Atlantic. He was following his prey at a distance, hanging well back and doing nothing aggressive that would alarm them and make them put into port.

"It seemed to work. The *Concepcion* did not put into port, which was unusual but convenient. She did not show any alarm or even awareness at being followed, but that may be because Halfbeard was clever and used some old tricks like dragging mattresses or anchors behind the *Calmare* to slow his ship down and make it look like she was just a small, heavily laden merchant vessel. He might well have kept the swivel guns shrouded as well. Still, I think the crew of the *Concepcion* may not have reacted to his presence for another reason."

"What reason?"

Ben shrugged. This didn't mean that he didn't know, just that he wasn't ready to lay his theory out for inspection. That meant it was something alarming and he probably wanted to talk me into letting him have the run of my records before I got upset.

The thought of all the letters and journals in my attic had Ben smacking his lips, but I was adamant about looking through things in my own time before turning anything over. This stubbornness made Harris Ladd happy. Ben was, after all, still an outsider and a writer, and therefore did not need to be privy to family secrets.

"This part of the story is especially sketchy. There are just a few notes made by a doctor who treated some sailors from the *Calmare* about a week later. I would really like to get some confirmation here."

"It's okay. I want to hear it."

"All right. Here is what I think happened. The crew of the *Concepcion* surrendered immediately when Halfbeard hoisted the Jolly Roger. Not a single shot was fired. One can't help but wonder if this was because they feared their cargo and wanted to be rid of it. Certainly they were very sick with something they called *Lepra de Mono*. Roughly translated it is *monkey leprosy*. I think it was these combined woes of the treasure and illness which distracted them and made them happy to give over their prize without a fight."

"But what was it? Golden idols? Water from the Fountain of Youth? What?"

Ben shook his head.

"I don't think so. The treasure, whatever it was, was divided among the crew of the *Calmare* and they sailed north. The *Concepcion* was not found until decades later when she washed up on a beach in South America. At least, we believe it was the

Concepcion. There was no one onboard—no bodies at any rate. But there was still food and drink in barrels and rotting clothing. When the crew left, if they left, they didn't take their possessions or provisions with them. Wood-eating shipworms had been at work without hindrance for many years and the anchor was gone as well as the prow of the ship. It was kind of like the *Mary Celeste*, if you know that story."

I remembered the story by Sir Arthur Conan Doyle. The *Mary Celeste* had been abandoned by her crew mid-meal and none of them were ever found. Most everyone assumed that they had been killed.

"You think Halfbeard murdered the crew when he robbed them? But wouldn't that be unusual since they surrendered? And why wouldn't he keep the ship, even if just to sell later?" My brain leapt to a lurid conclusion, not awaiting Ben's answer. "Because of the curse? Maybe his men wouldn't stay onboard to sail her?"

"Maybe. Or they were afraid of the disease that infected them. Maybe his men refused to sail a pestilent ship. Or he simply didn't have the crew to spare since he had to leave Tortuga de Mar so hastily. Obviously he didn't hole her or set her afire, which would have been standard practice if he wanted a ship to disappear."

"But you think Halfbeard killed the crew, even if he didn't touch the ship?" I insisted.

This bothered me though I knew it was silly to feel shame at what some distant ancestor had done.

"Maybe they were already dead by then. It's possible. It sounds as though this so called monkey plague was a brisk one." Ben cleared his throat and began using what I think of as his storyteller's voice. "Bad weather attended them as they sailed north and half the crew deserted or were put into hospitals when they put in at Charleston. I can't find any record of what was wrong with them. The doctor was baffled. It could have been scurvy coupled with something else. Or … who knows? The doctor certainly didn't. He had never heard of monkey leprosy."

"How long did it take to get to Charleston from Florida?"

"Only days. As I said, whatever disease was onboard the *Concepcion*, it was highly contagious. And here is the odd part, the sailors were all listed as indigents and ended up in pauper's graves, their corpses smothered with quicklime. This was a method for dealing with plague victims and also criminals, though there was no mention of the doctor knowing that these men were pirates. I think he did this as a health measure. And it worked because none of the nurses or servants who cleaned the hospital got sick."

I thought about this.

"Halfbeard wouldn't have paid for his crew's medical care or to have them buried? But why, when he had money?" This wasn't as silly as it sounded. Captains usually looked after loyal crew. It made it easier to find willing sailors if the captain was fair.

"He sailed before the men died. Whatever the treasure was, it wasn't standard gold or silver or jewels—or at least the sick didn't bring anything of value with them when they came on land. I think maybe they refused to bring anything. Maybe they thought they could beat the curse and get better if they got away from the ship and did not keep the treasure."

"But they died anyway."

"And the storm never ceased while the *Calmare* was in port."

I thought about this. Under my blouse my arms were chilled and the hairs were standing on end.

"They talked about the bad weather in Charleston?" Weather bad enough to mention and write down was bad weather indeed.

"Yes. It was an odd storm that covered only half the town. Like I said, I'm speculating here, but we know for sure that the fast-moving storm followed them up the coast and into Charleston. And then it moved on. It's noted in every port city where they stopped—stopped, but did not disembark. The storm definitely seemed to come and go with the *Calmare*."

"That's ... creepy."

"Finally they made it to our islands and the storm ended. Just cut off."

I exhaled. Caught up in the story, it was easy to imagine a battle of supernatural forces. Of course, it was more likely that the tropical storm just blew itself out. I needed to stop scaring myself. People back then looked first to supernatural explanations, but that didn't mean I had to.

"And Halfbeard somehow met Abercrombie's daughter and convinced her to marry him?" I sounded incredulous.

Ben nodded.

"This is where I am lacking documentation." Another barnacle came loose and shot across the floor. Kelvin ignored it but Barney galloped after it. I took it away at once, picking it up in a tea towel so I wouldn't have to touch it. I really needed to get some new tennis balls. I'd call Mrs. Sibley and see if she could add that to Tuesday's delivery.

"I wish I had a portrait of the man. His affect was said to be striking. And this was just five years before Blackbeard made his way into villainy's hall of fame. I don't know why history liked him better. Maybe it was the flaming hair. The man had a knack for drama."

"There is no portrait? Before or after his accident?" I asked and Ben grimaced.

"Not unless you have one in the house. Anyhow, he married two weeks later and then he turned the *Calmare* over to Darby and what was left of the crew. Two men opted to remain in Maine on the mainland. The rest accepted the offer of partnership in the *Calmare*. Maybe they thought they were safe because the storm had stopped. Or because Halfbeard had whatever part of the treasure they thought was cursed."

"So they waved goodbye to Little Goose and sailed south, and sank almost as soon as they were...." I stopped.

"Out of the islands' protection. Yes. Makes a good story, doesn't it? I just need some kind of proof that Halfbeard was actually Nicholas Wendover. Don't want people accusing me of slander without any basis in truth even if I am writing fiction. And there is no getting around the fact that this guy is a blot on the old family escutcheon."

He didn't mean me. The town folk tended to be touchy though. Especially when the stories were true. I didn't think they would like this tale regardless of his proofs.

"The family is nothing but blots."

Ben grinned.

"That's true, but this guy actually went out and earned his bad reputation."

"I'll look again for letters or a journal." Ben was always wanting me to look for stuff. I understood. Our library was a

16

treasure trove of information and local scandal. "There are still piles of books I need to go through. Maybe he kept a captain's log. If something's there I'll find it," I promised, feeling vaguely enthused. I love doing research and maybe this would give me something for my blog.

"I doubt—" But whatever he was skeptical about wasn't mentioned. The box popped open, almost as if it were spring-loaded, and we stared down at what I thought were a pair of gold coins and some brown sticks.

"Jesus wept," Ben breathed. He started to reach for the coins but stopped himself. "Do you know what these are?"

"Gold doubloons," I guessed.

"Close. These are what are commonly called pieces of eight. Minted in Mexico and not Seville. Regular kind were worth about eight shillings or say four hundred and fifty bucks each."

"These aren't regular?"

"No. Pieces of eight were made of silver. There have been only a few of these gold coins ever found and they have a rather sinister nickname."

"What?"

"Pieces of hate."

I stared at him.

"Why?"

"See those spear things?" He pointed but did not touch. I didn't know if this was to avoid getting oil on them—pristine coins are worth more to collectors than ones that have been touched—or if he simply didn't want to touch the shiny bits of ill will. "They should have been pillars, and on the other side, the lion has been replaced by a snake. The man who minted them was supposedly some kind of descendant of an Incan wizard. He sent the coins to the capitol as a kind of death threat. He also hated King Phillip V, who was actually French. You have to remember that the French pirates had been throwing their weight around down there almost as much as the Spanish navy were and were just as hated. Anyway, supposedly those who received the coins sickened and died. Of course, everyone sickened and died back then. Disease was rampant. He didn't last long in his career. They were still burning witches back then and the superstitious bastards barbecued him after the standard tortures."

I shuddered, feeling ill, and wondered that Ben could sound so glib when he spoke of such awful things.

"But they look so clean. And look at the box. The hinges aren't rusted. It can't be that old."

"Gold doesn't tarnish," Ben said slowly, but he began to frown.

"But they look so *new*. Can they be real? Maybe they are reproductions. Are they dated?"

"The earliest coins have no date." Ben exhaled. "I don't know. I wonder what those brown—oh."

"What?"

"Don't get upset. But those brown things are bones."

I stared at them. They were bones. Finger bones. Very small finger bones.

"Oh God! Not...."

"No! No, of course not. They are probably monkey bones. They would have put the paw in as a … sort of talisman. Like a lucky rabbit's foot."

"Monkey leprosy," I muttered. "For heavensake, close the box and don't touch anything. I can't believe it's real." Except a part of me did believe it. "But if it is, well, we can't risk contagion until it's checked out."

Ben closed the box. He looked pale. I guess the whole thing was getting very real for him.

"Tess, monkey leprosy probably had nothing to do with monkeys or leprosy. They weren't medical geniuses back then. They just fixed blame on whatever was handy."

"I know. But let's be safe, okay? You have open wounds on your hands. In fact, you'd better wash them and get some antibiotic ointment on them. They could get infected."

The tea kettle finally began shrieking. I was glad of an excuse to turn away from the box.

"Shouldn't the bones have rotted?" I asked. "I mean we are talking about something at least two hundred and fifty, maybe three hundred years old. If it's what you think it is."

"Or older, so you would think so. Tess?"

"Yes." I busied myself with making the tea.

"I know it's a lot to ask, but would it be okay if I took these artifacts to a friend at the maritime museum? He's discreet and Michael knows a lot more than I do about—everything. He will be able to date things so we can know what we're dealing with. I am probably just leaping to conclusions because I'm caught up in research and want this box to belong to Nicholas Wendover. But this could be anything. I mean, is it likely that a pirate would throw out gold coins?"

If he was leaping to conclusions then I was diving right behind him. But unlike Ben, I could easily imagine someone being willing to part with gold if it would save their life.

Still, was this something I should let out of my sight? It seemed to have been rather directed at me. And this box and its horrid contents were probably worth a lot of money.

I looked at Ben. It is sometimes difficult to know a person when there are lots of distractions around them, like an exotic career or lots of money. But I had gotten pretty good at spotting the villains no matter what they camouflaged themselves with and I didn't think Ben was one of them.

"Fine by me. At least for a little while." And I meant that. I wanted the horrid box out of the house and off the island while I sorted out what to do. "You'll warn your friend about the bones and the sickness and everything?"

"Of course." Suddenly he abandoned his gloom and broke into a grin. "By God, Tess! If this isn't a hoax…. We'll be making history. I'll get a bestseller out of it for sure. And you'll be rich. Who knows what those coins are worth! The last one was sold at auction back in the fifties and it went for forty thousand."

I nodded, trying to be enthused. It was difficult though. The storm that had brought the box up on the beach had not been normal and the light around it—probably some kind of Saint Elmo's fire—had felt unnatural. The story behind the box was also pretty awful and involved supernatural agencies. Assuming the box and my ancestor pirate were related to one another, and I had a bad feeling that they were. How else would an Incan magician's *pieces of hate* get to Maine?

Something began to nibble on the back of my brain.

"Ben, when did you say the boat sank?"

"The *Calmare*? During the night on either September ninth or early on the tenth."

"Do you know what day it is?" I asked, my flesh going goose-bumpy again.

"Um—I guess…." Ben was a writer and didn't keep close track of the days or even months. He knew it was Tuesday or Friday if he heard the ferry. It was winter if there was snow.

"September tenth. What year did it sink?"

"Well … 1712. Wow. That is just uncanny." I knew he was only thinking about how good the coincidence would be for his book. He wasn't appreciating how sinister the timing was and I didn't want to say what I was thinking out loud.

"Have you got a camera?" Ben asked. "We need to take some pictures. I wish I had done it before I pried the box open."

The box had probably never been pretty, but its sojourn in the sea and subsequent encrustation had not improved it.

"Don't worry. I took pictures already."

"Good. Get your camera. Let's take some more. I want a record of everything."

Chapter 2

*My wife, her maid, the outdoor lad and the cook have no
knowledge of reckoning proper time. I have set them on watches
for the Dog, the First and the Mid. My wife insisted that we do not
ring the bell to avoid rousing those who sleep, but I wake in time
for every eight bell and walk the house to see for myself that all is
well.*
        —from the unbound journal of *Halfbeard*

We took more pictures of the chest, and I uploaded them to
my computer and emailed copies to Ben. Then, at his insistence, I
called Harris and told him what I had found and asked about
insurance. As I had expected, Harris said we probably couldn't
take out insurance until we knew what we had, but to mail him
copies of the pictures and that he would make enquiries. He
assured me that until I sold the box—assuming I did, which I knew
Harrison would never approve of—I didn't need to worry about
entering anything in the Doomsday Book.
    Taxes were the last thing on my mind.
    I agreed to do as Harris asked and hung up quietly. I was
feeling uneasy. Perhaps because Harris was also uneasy, though he
tried to hide it from me. My attorney is a creature of ritual and
habit—and schedule. It would not surprise me to learn that he
walked in widdershins circles and bayed to the moon before
getting into bed. He is a traditionalist whose beliefs are repackaged
eighteenth-century superstitions. He probably believes in cursed
treasure. And he wouldn't be alone in this if word got out. Strange
boxes appearing on the beach during unnatural storms is just part
of the local microclimate of weirdness that happens in the islands.
    And because of that, I didn't really want word getting out
about pirate treasure—cursed or otherwise. I knew Harris and Ben
would keep quiet. Harris didn't want strangers on the island and
Ben didn't want anyone scooping him on his story. But was the
curator at the museum someone who would be able to keep quiet in
the face of a great discovery? And what about my insurance agent?
    Who the hell was my agent? I was annoyed to find out that I
didn't know. He had likely been Kelvin's agent—my great-

grandfather, not the cat. I just had to hope that he was trustworthy too.

As promised, I began searching for letters, journals, and diaries. I looked through the history books as well, hoping that there would be something in them, some mention of Halfbeard by an enterprising writer a century back. It was slow going. I was careful not to touch any of the taxidermy I had to work around. If I left them undisturbed, I wouldn't have to smell them. As much. My least favorite of the preserved corpses was a ridiculously large varnished swordfish. I don't care for maritime decorations, especially dead ones that stink.

Barney galloped by, stirring up dust. Almost instantly I began sneezing, violent paroxysms that nearly caused whiplash and left my head aching.

"This place needs cleaning. Maybe I should tie dustcloths to the pair of you and let you chase mice."

Kelvin looked at me with scorn but Barney wagged his cobwebbed tail. He has a hopeful disposition and thought maybe this would be a fun game.

The attic was stuffy and unbearable past eleven, so after a superficial look inside the latest filthy box which looked fairly promising, I grabbed it and another small crate of papers and dragged it down to the library where I could work in the cool and comfort.

The cool and comfort weren't enough to keep me on point. My ancestors may have had many skills that I am unaware of, but I think I can safely say that there was not a closet librarian among them, except perhaps my great-grandfather, Kelvin. And he arranged his books by some system unknown to adherents of either Dewy Decimal or alphabetizing. And no one had made any effort to straighten loose papers which seemed to have been heaped in whatever chest or crate was available and stuffed in the attic with no thought of tidiness or that someone might actually wish to examine the writings someday. A few personal letters were sometimes tied up with ribbon, but these were usually romantic missives and a century off of the date I was searching for.

"Maybe there was some emergency," I said to Kelvin. "Like a flood and they just rushed to get everything to higher ground before it was destroyed."

This seemed unlikely though. What might have happened was someone making a frantic search for something and not having the time or inclination to clean up afterwards; they had just stuffed things in boxes higgledy-piggledy and dumped them in the attic.

"Doesn't matter how it happened, I suppose. It has to be sorted." I sighed and Barney sighed too. There would be no playing for a while.

Things started going into piles by date—when I had one—and by name when I did not, though this was hardly satisfactory given that almost all my male ancestors had been named Kelvin. Eventually my body announced that my eyes would herniate if I read and sorted any longer. The angel on my shoulder—the not so good one—suggested that I had done my neighborly duty and that I needed some fresh air to resuscitate the brain cells.

It would come as a surprise to most people who know me, but once in a while my better sense is overcome by the need for a seasonal craft project. Stepping out to look at my small back garden, I decided that I would leave the largest of the garden sunflowers to set seed for the birds in winter and that the smaller ones needed to be cut and dried for an autumnal wreath.

"Come on, guys," I said to Kelvin and Barney. "Let's get some sun."

It was technically still summer, but the first pangs of autumn were in the air and my sleeveless shirt was probably a little optimistic. You could feel the changing season on the skin and smell it in the wind. It made Barney joyous and Kelvin sleepy.

"I should cut back the Virginia creeper." Or have someone come and cut it back. The transplant had proven a ferocious contender for most dominant plants and was fighting a fierce battle with the English ivy for control of the back porch. The curtain was thick enough to create a kind of twilight.

However, the creeper looked like a big job that might need a ladder since it had grown up onto the wall. I decided to save it for later and began clipping sunflowers, trying to enjoy the breeze and the sun that warmed my back. Though the weather was very pleasant, I couldn't shake the feeling that something unpleasant was looming large. Larger than usual. Closer. I had a weird kind of faith that the islands would protect me from whatever outside threat was approaching. But it still felt like it was my obligation to be rid of the hostile invader if I could manage it since it might be a threat to others. Also, unfinished business can trouble spirits that should be at rest. Those swindled in life can be nasty in death, as I had cause to know.

There was nothing new about this idea. I had been tying up my ancestors' loose ends since I arrived on the island.

In an attempt to push back the mental shadows I began humming *Jesu, Joy of Man's Desiring,* sadly with more enthusiasm than accuracy. Barney and Kelvin didn't mind my version of Bach and the composer was dead, so who cared if I flatted a note or two?

I hadn't been at work for more than a few minutes when Mary Cory arrived. I wondered what she wanted. It seemed doubtful that one of her rare moments of friendliness was visiting her since she had smiled at me only last week.

"That almost sounded like Bach."

I don't dislike anyone with sufficient fervor to spend a lot of valuable brain wattage hating them by the hour, but Mary isn't my favorite person and seeing her had the potential to ruin the day.

"Delibes," I lied.

Neither of my pets rushed over to see her. She isn't an animal person and they know it.

Mary takes care of an aging neighbor, Archibald Hicks, who owns one of the two other houses on the island. Archibald is so very old that he has begun to blur around the edges. Old age and illness have consumed his vitality and I always feel I need to be ready to run over and resuscitate him. His muscles and memory sagged long ago, skin and hair have faded to beige and he looks like a watercolor portrait of himself that had been painted on cheap tissue paper which has begun to disintegrate. Though no one has said it straightly, I believe that he lives on the island because he thinks that it somehow prolongs his life, that the island keeps death away. Though what he goes on living for I cannot guess. He rarely has visitors and there is no other family that anyone knows about.

24

Mary doesn't wear a nurse's uniform on the job, but even her summer sandals somehow manage to look sober and orthopedic. They matched her nature, which has had the slightly grim island culture ground into it like some kind of invisible tattoo that can't be seen by outsiders but whose irritating presence can be felt. I think the muscles for laughter have atrophied and she looks rather like an old person is living behind her younger face and always forcing it into a worried frown even when there is no particular reason for concern.

The islands are kind of inbred and everyone who has lived here through the centuries has broad, overlapping interests and relationships. Sometimes deciding which role to play could be confusing and involved splitting hairs so fine they could only be seen with an electron microscope. My family, in particular, has had a long and strange relationship with the other islanders. Thanks to our familial curse—or blessing—I have an undeniable degree of local notoriety. Some people fear me because of my lineage. Others love me for being their savior. I deserve neither fear nor love from these people who are still virtual strangers, but that's just how it is.

Mary is an exception. She neither fears nor loves me. We tolerate one another when we must interact and ignore each other when we can. Apparently this wasn't one of the days when we could pretend the other didn't exist.

I tucked my flower into the bucket and then turned fully to face her. Best not to draw things out. Goodwill can curdle quickly and I wanted to answer her questions and send her on her way rejoicing. Or not.

The first thing I noticed was that she had colored half her hair a strange shade of red that looked like it had come from a spray can. In fact, as I looked closer I could see flecks of red on her old sweatshirt. Knowing it was paint and not blood was a relief though I had to wonder how she had gotten it in her hair.

Mary has an unusual hobby. She makes *papier-mâché* figurines of people's deceased pets. I find it a bit strange but certainly more agreeable than the taxidermy that fills my attic. Still, she is about as witty a conversationalist as one of Barney's squeak toys and I avoid her lectures when I can.

As usual, she was scowling slightly and her mouth was pulled into a frown. I didn't take it personally. The only time she didn't scowl was when she was with Everett Sands. Everett and his brother, Bryson, are the local law. Bryson is charming. Everett less so, and I think he is with Mary mostly because she will never punch him in the brain with her intellect. Both of the brothers are smugglers who used to use my great-grandfather's hidden sea cave and secret staircase for smuggling whisky from Canada—with his blessing, I should add. In the islands we all kind of live outside the law, if that can be said of people who have probably never been inside of it to begin with.

And, just to complicate things, one of their ancestors was also responsible for hanging one of mine. It was a love affair that ended in accusations of witchcraft, which sometimes happened in New England back in the seventeenth and eighteenth centuries. I have been willing to forgive, but forgetting is harder for all of us, especially when there are ghosts who refuse to rest.

Like I said, it's all kind of inbred and every time I saw Bryson I had to decide if he was there as the law or a smuggler, to be hated for an ancient wrong done to an innocent woman or considered as a potential romantic partner.

And Mary.... How did she fit in? Her presence was suspicious so soon after the box's arrival. Could Everett have sent her?

"Do you have a stud finder I can borrow?" she asked. These were not the words I expected.

I resisted the urge to make any jokes about her finding studs. Mary has no sense of humor and I didn't really want to know what she was doing. At least, I didn't want to know from her. I would ask Bryson later. Unlike Everett and Mary, he wasn't witheringly unimaginative. If he didn't know the truth he would make up an entertaining lie.

"No, but Ben might. He's been hanging shelves and pictures." Ben's office is functional, full of filing cabinets and, except for his chair, lacking in comfortable furniture. He had decided to add some shelves and hang some of his awards. I like my library more, though I will grant that Ben's office, devoid of cushions and pets, is probably better at keeping a body focused on their work.

Mary shook her head.

"He's gone to the mainland. Took off going wicked fast earlier this morning."

Probably with the chest and high hopes of fame and fortune. Well, that suited me fine. The damned box gave me the willies.

"I have a small tool chest, but it's just hammers and screwdrivers, I think. Do you want to look through it?" I had to make some gesture of helpfulness. Only four of us live on the island. It is important to be on good terms.

"No. I'll call Everett. Damn," she muttered. "I wonder why Ben left. He was here earlier, wasn't he? Did he say anything about leaving?"

So, she had been watching the house. She couldn't need a stud finder that badly, could she?

"Yes. He's got me looking through old family letters. He's trying to find some information on one of the Wendovers for a book he's doing and he is all riled up about it."

"Which one of your ancestors?" Mary asked, trying to be casual. Mary doesn't read much and has no interest in genealogy.

"The one who married Abercrombie's daughter. The ship captain from away."

"Ah." She nodded. Apparently my failure to use the word pirate had reassured her. Mary is one of those who doesn't like the ugly old facts disturbed by research. "Quite a storm we had last night."

"Yes. I wasn't expecting it."

"Have you been down to the beach today?" she asked abruptly.

I stared at her, trying to decide if this was her version of small talk or if Mary was actually trying to be sly.

"Is there any good driftwood?" I answered without answering. "I wouldn't mind a piece for a flower arrangement I have in mind."

"I don't know." She paused. "I haven't gone down to the beach. I'm too busy. Maybe Ben went down."

This new thought made her frown.

"Oh. Well, I may walk down later and have a look around." I turned back to my tidy row of sunflowers and began snipping. "See you," I said.

27

"Bye." I heard her walk away.

"Well, that was strange," I muttered to Kelvin. "Do you think she knows something about the chest?"

Kelvin meowed.

"I think so too. Maybe she just saw Ben rushing off with it and got curious enough to come for a visit."

But I suspected it was more than that. I bet she had heard rumors of treasure through the years and it had probably excited her interest. Gold had that effect on many people. However, there was nothing I could do about what she thought so I shook my head and went back to cutting flowers.

Eventually I returned to my boxes of paper and found many interesting things, but nothing from Nicholas Wendover and no captain's logs entitled *The Diary of Halfbeard the Pirate*.

Night hadn't reached the west side of the island when Barney began to pace and whine, but the increasing shadows in the east made me nervous. My limbic brain had become sensitized to certain stimuli and it could not ignore the circumstances under which the box had arrived. It was off island with Ben, who still hadn't returned or I would have seen lights at his house, so I should have felt safe. But I didn't. The coming storm was hostile.

Finally I drew the curtains against the sunset and resisted the urge to go downstairs and check yet again that both outside doors as well as the one to the basement and the secret stair were locked. They were. I had already checked. Twice.

I decided on a bath though tremendous effort is needed to coax the aged taps into opening and releasing the dangerously hot water created by the immersion heater mounted in an old brass tank. I would have liked it better if the cistern screamed like a tea kettle when it was ready instead of relying on a timer which had rust around the edges, but the damn thing worked fine and they hadn't made a water heater large enough to supply water for the giant old bathtub. So, I took life in hand once again and I turned on the heater and went to make hot chocolate.

After I had boiled myself a nice shade of lobster, I gathered up Barney and Kelvin and retired upstairs where I lit a fire in the bedroom grate. It wasn't cold, but a fire is friendly and there is comfort in light that won't go out if a line or transformer goes down.

I was not surprised when I heard the storm begin its angry symphony. The moaning of the wind could be heard above the crackling in the grate and the sound cut right through the calm well-being provided by the hot bath and cocoa.

I love the house and have always felt welcome and safe here. Usually it doesn't seem empty because I had never lived here with anyone else so don't know any differently. But something about that night made the rooms fill up with the awareness that my family was dead and I was entirely alone and vulnerable.

Kelvin mewed and smacked my leg with his claws. The tiny pain broke my bleak reverie and I again felt fine. The room was just a room. The fireplace would be warm and inviting as soon as I laid some kindling in the hearth.

Barney got in his bed and huddled unhappily until I gave in and called him up on the mattress. Kelvin got up on my pillow and stared at the bedroom door while I finished laying the fire.

My knees were stiff as I got to my feet and crossed the room to the window where the rain tapped with impatient fingers. The curtains were heavy and resisted drawing back as if they didn't want me looking out at the night. I insisted and eventually stared out of the narrow opening in the fabric and saw that the wind was rearranging my yard, decorating it with loose leaves and twigs and pulling the seed heads off dying shrubs. Almost the instant I drew the curtain aside, the wind began attacking the glass from different directions as though trying to find a way inside and when thwarted, punishing me by cutting off my line of sight with blown leaves and debris. I told myself that this was like watching a horror movie with really high production values. The thought didn't make me feel any better.

The house shivered, as though it were aware of outside danger and quaking on its foundations.

Locals think that I control the weather, but I don't.

I let the curtain fall shut and turned back to my four-legged friends.

"Let's read," I said to Kelvin, who didn't bother to look away from the door though Barney wagged his tail hopefully. He likes when I talk to him.

I knew what Kelvin wanted. He likes to roam the house at night, but this was one of the times when I wanted my door closed and locked against the dark and storm.

Chapter 3

In our hearts we knew tempest impended and the crew grew gloomy in mynd. Every nyght when evening came and the storm grew even darker, a strange cloud of mist would form about the ship. It affrighted me and the men and we always made to outrun it. We kept watch at all tymes, burning the oil for the lamps most recklessly because we feared the dark.
—from the unbound journal of *Halfbeard*

Ben was just back from the mainland at first light and excited enough to call. The joy was because his friend was doing tests to confirm that the box, the bones, and the gold were all what they thought they were.

I tried for an encouraging tone but it was hard when I had no coffee, and I was aware that in my distraction over the box I had forgotten to call and add it to the grocery order that was being delivered. Ben finally admitted that he hadn't slept and could use a nap, so we wrapped things up and I went to make some tea.

Hearing the ferry only a short time later and being recalled to the present reality of an empty larder, I grabbed my purse and hurried for the dock. I wasn't really pulled together, but we don't have a lot of fashion plates in the islands and all the basic grooming was covered.

Barney was following closely as he always does, so I detoured by Ben's, hoping he wasn't asleep already.

I climbed up Ben's path and stuck my head in the open door and called to him, asking if Barney could stay while I made a coffee run.

A bleary-eyed Ben agreed but then asked, "Isn't that the ferry now?"

"Yes, and I forgot to add coffee to my order. I've got to catch a ride now. If you are sure Barney won't keep you up."

"Oh well, in an emergency I can make do, right, dog?" Anyway, he looks like he needs a nap." He smiled at Barney who thumped his tail.

"Thanks!"

Barney, who is used to staying with Ben, didn't follow me to the docks.

I groped for my sunglasses. The morning sky was low and a bit hard on the eyes. The directionless haze glared painfully as the sun slowly gnawed its way through the obstinate clouds. I thought it looked like a migraine headache.

I was also repelled by the strange-looking seaweed that was draped along the path. The storm had to have brought it ashore, but how hard did a wind have to blow to force rotting vegetation up a stony path?

"Captain Sibley," I said, managing a smile for him though I knew none would be returned. "Just leave the parcels on the dock. We'll get them later. I need a ride into Goose Haven, if you'll have me."

"Ayuh? Come aboard then."

Our conversations always scintillated.

I had a few bad moments on the ride to Goose Haven and admit that I wouldn't have been surprised if a kraken had risen up from the deep and attacked us, but of course nothing happened. My subconscious was certain though that some tide had shifted. And not for the better. For the first time since I had come to the islands I was afraid, not just cautious, of the ocean. Samuel Johnston came to mind. It was his opinion that being on a ship was like being in jail only with the added hazard of drowning.

The theme of my thoughts was insistently recurrent. Certainly these were not waters I wanted to go swimming in, so I stayed back from the rail and hummed Bach under my breath.

The humming helped, but the unease never quite left me and it was a relief to get land under my legs again. I headed for Mike's chowder house with enthusiasm. I was looking for Bryson and knew that since it was Tuesday he was likely there for lunch. They get their blueberry pies on Monday afternoon and it is better after it has had a chance to *set* overnight.

I was also in luck because Mike had just taken his various barbecued sea bugs off the menu and the seafood and charcoal smog that surrounded the chowder house in August had abated. You didn't have to like shellfish to live here, but to avoid eating it was seen as shirking one's civic duty. Now all I had to avoid was the breakfast special of fishcakes and hot donuts. If worse came to worst, there was always cabbage soup, the most exotic thing on the menu year round and sometimes the only thing without fish.

Tuesday isn't a popular day for lunching out so the chowder house wasn't busy. In fact, it was about as lively as a funeral parlor, I thought, and then almost tripped over my own feet when I saw who was dining there. Other than Bryson the only other customer was Jonas Traynor who runs a mortuary on the mainland. He looks very New England—lean, standing straight as a church steeple and pointing the way to heaven. There is another undertaker in the islands but the Catholics prefer to use Jonas. That he was on Great Goose instead of in his parlor likely meant that someone of that faith had died.

I cast my mind back to the latest gossip and recalled that old Mrs. Tudor had been sick with pneumonia. I knew her slightly, mostly because of her volunteer work at the museum and intense menthol smell that always followed her. No one else was ill and I had heard nothing of any accidents, so it probably was Elmira Tudor who had departed this vale of Vicks VapoRub.

"Miss MacKay." He nodded once with great solemnity.

"Mister Traynor."

We exchanged nods but didn't shake hands or—heaven forbid—hug. People around here didn't as a rule and that was a relief.

Of course, I couldn't actually smell death on him, but seeing Traynor in his quasi-religious garb and perpetually grim face caused a certain low-level anxiety which I didn't need, being full up on things to be anxious about already. Hopefully coffee and Bryson's calm presence would override my imagination which insisted the cold odor of the mortuary was condensing on the back of my neck as I walked away from the undertaker.

"Tess," Bryson acknowledged as I joined him at his table which was hovered over by a fishing net and an antique lobster cage. The remains of a bowl of chowder sat in front of him. He looked pleased but not especially surprised to see me. Which he should have been, since I don't usually leave the island on Tuesdays and certainly not to go to the chowder house for lunch.

"Mrs. Tudor?" I asked softly, jerking my head in Traynor's direction.

Bryson nodded.

"Yes, she passed last night during the storm. Poor thing was delirious with fever and raving about pirate ships."

I shuddered at the unexpected words. Bryson saw this and raised a brow.

"Poor thing," I said. "Not an easy passing then. Was Father Hanlon there?"

"No. The storm was too bad so she had no one there to keep the evil at bay—except Reverend Burnes, of course, but the family didn't send for him."

Burnes or visions of pirates. Talk about being caught between the devil and the deep blue sea. Personally, I thought they had made the right choice.

Bryson offered me the newspaper he was reading but I declined. Anything except the local made the outside world sound like it was locked into a death spiral. And maybe it was, but since there was nothing I could do about it, I preferred blissful ignorance.

"I don't blame you," he said, folding it up and laying it aside. "It's all depressing. Frankly, I can't believe you used to own a newspaper. It would probably make me slit my wrists seeing all that bad news on my desk first thing in the morning."

I didn't think his desk at the station could be covered in good news, but said nothing about that.

"It wasn't a very good newspaper. In fact, it had no news at all. People preferred it that way."

We had discussed this matter before. It seemed like our country had been infected with some autoimmune disease (greed and fear) that first made the government (lackeys of wealthy corporations) attack society and then society attack itself. And none of us wanted to admit that the damned disease had metastasized and was getting worse, so we lived on the surface and grew ever more distant from each other even though every month we were offered more options for our phones and internet. After all, though we ate the same breakfast cereal, wore the same jeans, and listened to Nat King Cole at Christmas, someone living in the heart of big-city urban blight wouldn't have the same kinds of thoughts and worries as a farmer facing drought in the Midwest. Some people had to worry about gangbangers and drugs killing their children, others worried about crop circles and alien invasions of the outer-space variety killing their cows and corn. Hawaii isn't Minnesota. New Mexico isn't New Hampshire. And none of them were a coastal island in Maine where people still believed in sea monsters and pirates. Our experiment in national unity was falling apart. The technologies of television and the internet that were supposed to bring us together were instead pushing us apart with lies and mass hysteria.

Not that they were completely unified on every front here in the islands. There are folks who eat and drink the usual racist swill and store it up in the unventilated chambers of their narrow minds, but much more than skin color or religion, the location and family of your birth are what matters. To them, Catholics like Mr. Traynor and Mrs. Tudor would always be outsiders though the families had been there a century and more.

"I did want to be nosy about something else though, if you have the time."

Bryson's lips twitched.

"Go ahead and take a pew. I am always available to the public."

I tucked myself in to the booth and thought about what to ask. I decided not to lead with the storm and the creepy chest left on the beach. It tied in a little too well with Mrs. Tudor's delirium.

"What the heck is Mary doing that she has bright red paint in her hair and needs a stud finder?"

Bryson chuckled. "I'm tempted to make up something here. The real answer is kind of mundane."

"If you make it up it'll have to be good because I already have placed her in an S&M parlor with one of those sex swings."

"Mary Cory in a sex swing? Your imagination is better than mine. And speaking of imagination, Tess...."

He wasn't going to let me off the hook.

"Yes, it was a freaky storm," I said. "Two freaky storms. No, I didn't cause them—didn't even know they were coming. Yes, there was a box on the beach and it might have belonged to a

35

pirate. No, I don't have it. Ben's taken it to a maritime museum to make sure it isn't a fake."

Bryson frowned at me.

"In another era—"

"They'd hang me for a witch," I finished. We had both been thinking of Miss Marple and *The Murder at the Vicarage*, but since I had an ancestor who had been hanged for a witch, the reference was ill-chosen. "Is there anything you want to tell me, any colorful stories about the pirate who married into the family that Harris might have forgotten to mention and Ben hasn't dug up yet?"

Bryson hesitated.

"Was he a pirate? I've always wondered if the stories were true. Kind of hoped they weren't, given some of the legends."

That wasn't promising.

"Ben sure thinks they're true. He has me pouring through the attic's boxes of books and papers looking for proof that Nicholas Wendover was some pirate called Halfbeard."

Bryson shook his head.

"What are you going to do about the box? If it's real?"

"Need I do anything about it?" I asked. "Why not just keep it?"

Bryson raised a brow.

I wanted to stare him down but he was right, something would have to be done eventually if the thing was the genuine article. I couldn't stand the creepy feeling I had when the sun went down and the wind began to blow, which I feared it would keep doing as long as the box was around. And the box itself was made of some concentrated repellant. "First I need to find out what is really going on with the damned thing because it just doesn't feel like a regular old box to me. Did Kelvin know about the thing?" And the pieces of hate within it?

"Well...." Bryson hesitated, glancing around the restaurant. A man in law enforcement, wearing a gun, should not look that nervous.

My brain began leaping to conclusions. This box thing had probably happened before. Like when my grandmother still lived here? Had it been part of the reason that my grandmother fled the island? I didn't know the exact date she left, only that it was at the end of September. The timing was suspicious though I suppose she might just have wanted to beat the winter so her escape would not be dogged with weather disasters.

And Kelvin? Had he faked his death and fled for the same reason? Had he feared this anniversary enough to flee it? I had thought that I had his disappearing act figured out, but maybe not.

"I think he knew, though he never said anything directly. I think whenever it washed up—every decade or so—he just chucked it back again and then he'd go on a three-day drunk." I stared at Bryson, trying to recall what I'd asked. The box—right. Had Kelvin known about it?

"But it keeps coming back?" I asked unhappily.

"Yes. Apparently so."

"Did he open it? Did he say what was inside?"

"He never said anything to me. Or Everett. That I know of. I'll talk to my brother tonight. He was closer to your great-grandfather than I was and maybe Everett had the truth out of him."

"Hmph."

There was an awful lot that my great-grandfather hadn't said about all kinds of things I really needed to know. And as for the truth, especially the old truths, it was usually not that obvious or easily found. Around here it was an elusive commodity, hiding itself in shadowy nooks and crannies where it was hard to find.

I would be surprised to hear that Kelvin had confided anything in Everett Sands though. Bryson's brother was utterly amoral in the service of his own desires and interests and my great-grandfather knew this. In fact, I had to wonder if Bryson actually liked his brother.

"So, from this we could conclude that either the box wants to be on land, or the return offerings Kelvin made weren't being accepted." I paused, thinking. "Because something was wrong with the way he did it, or with him. Maybe he wasn't the right person to deal with the box." Bryson waited for me to go on. "Or something is wrong with the box itself, or with what's in it. Or because there's some ritual for box-chucking that I don't know about, but which must be followed." The list was getting long and I felt frustrated.

37

"Ayuh. You or anyone else."

"I sure hope it isn't a case of needing to track down all the coins the crew spent after they robbed that ship, because it can't be done. Not after all this time."

"Coins?"

But even as I said this, I wondered if that were true. Ben said that the ship had only let crew ashore once before it made it to Maine and that was for the sailors taken to the hospital in Charleston. Indigent ones, Ben said, who had no coins to pay for their medicine and ended up in pauper's graves. Had all the rest of the treasure still been aboard the *Calmare* when it went down? Or thrown overboard before then, if the crew came to believe that the coins and they were cursed?

"I can see thoughts spinning like tops in your head," Bryson said. "It's attractive in a weird way but rather scares me too."

"Who me? I never think. About tops anyway."

"Just be careful, Tess, and call me if you get nervous being alone out there. I have a spare room you can use anytime."

I have noticed, when trouble comes around to visit, a distinct lack of inclination from the men in my life to offer services any more emphatic in nature than the opportunity to sleep in their spare bedroom or to recommend a good electrician, etc. Not there is much they can do under the strange circumstances that trouble usually manifests itself, but every now and again I forget that I like being a strong, independent woman and wish that some man would take me in his arms and say *there, there, little lady. Let me take care of this for you.* After all, nothing in my previous life had prepared me for dealing with possibly cursed treasure.

"Thanks. But I don't think that I'm in any danger. Not since Ben and his friend have the box somewhere else."

"I wouldn't be too sure of that, Tess. Seems to me your great-grandfather was plenty scared when that thing turned up and Kelvin knew a lot more about what was going on than anyone else."

Actually, I wasn't all that sure I was safe. Hadn't I been near panic the whole trip to Great Goose? What if part of the treasure was still in the house and the whatever it was wanted it back? How on earth would I find a small coin or coins if they were hidden?

Truth wasn't the only elusive thing on the island. A lot of concealed rooms and compartments had been found when I had the electrical wiring done, but there were probably a lot more forgotten secrets hidden in Wendover House.

Mike finally wandered over and we ordered blueberry pie and coffee.

"Mike, I think you need a swordfish for the wall. I'll bring you one."

He grinned. His deeply trenched face was working on some new smile lines.

"No thanks. Kelvin left it here for a while but I had to send it back. People were complaining about the smell. Put them right off their suppers, it did."

So much for that idea.

"Need a ride home?" Bryson asked. He was smiling again. "The ferry is long gone by now."

"Yes. If you don't mind my stopping at the store first. I need some coffee and tennis balls. Poor Barney is so desperate for things to play with that he has taken to chasing barnacles."

Bryson chuckled.

"The shifts some of us are put to."

"And I better get Kelvin some catnip or I'll never hear the end of it."

Bryson picked up the check. He's old fashioned that way.

"Tess," he asked as we stepped out into the headache haze, "do you think we're going to have another storm tonight?"

I opened my mouth to insist yet again that I had no control over the weather but changed my mind about what I was going to say.

"Maybe. And if there is, it might be a good thing if no one was out in it." I said this pointedly since Bryson and Everett made periodic whisky runs into Canada.

"Okay. I'll pass the word to stay off the water."

It only occurred to me later that he might not mean that he would call his brother and delay their whisky run, but that he would also put the word out among the fishermen.

"It's a good thing that you aren't a timid woman."

No, I'm not timid. But I am not insanely brave either. And sometimes it would be nice to pretend that I am a little timid so someone else could be courageous.

Chapter 4

The sun was lost in leaden vapor and the wynd was sullen and winter cold. Belatedly I was smote with remorse for my avarice, but repentant as I was there came no forgyvness and my acts lived in my mynd with the frytful vitality of a present evyl deed. The storm built itself around the greed and shameful fear which made me murder those wretches before my crew.
　　—from the unbound journal of *Halfbeard*

It didn't take more than a glimpse of a bottle of cognac to convince me that Bryson deserved a reward for bringing me home since he was protecting and serving above and beyond the call of duty. But it would have to be a short reward. I didn't want anyone on the water after dark and not just because it might storm. I had a creepy-crawly feeling at the back of my neck.

Catnip, check. Coffee, check. No tennis balls, but a Kong—check. And cognac, big, big check. I also decided to try one of Blu Barry's Truffles, though technically they shouldn't be called truffles because of the conglomeration of nuts and candied "blu barrys" coagulated in a rather dubious nougat.

The canned goods I ignored. Though I know that they are not actually old enough to have reached a state of decay, they still manage to give that impression. It must be the light that makes everything on the shelves appear dusty and faded, but I have no interest in eating anything that looks old enough and dented enough to have traveled in Paul Revere's saddlebags.

The younger Mrs. Mickle filled me in on the local gossip as she rang me up. Slowly. Though showing the early signs of senility, she was still the self-appointed record keeper of illegitimate births and marital infidelities. Not that she was inclined to ignore any other kind of misdeed, mayhem, or strangeness that happened in her realm. Mrs. Tudor's piratical death vision got a full and probably greatly embellished telling, and I couldn't escape until she had gnawed the story to the bone though I very much wanted to avoid hearing about it again.

"There aren't any *whys* without *becauses*," she finished and tapped the counter with a calloused finger. "Mark my words." And then she was off again.

I think I gasped in the right places but didn't add anything at the end of the performance except that I thought it might be coming on rain that night and hoped no one would be abroad. Mrs. Mickle's eyes got very big and she nodded solemnly.

I had a vision of my own as I stepped out of the shop, so clear it passed for divine—or perhaps diabolical—insight. There was a mass of clouds rolling in on the islands like giant boulders thundering down a mountain and the sun was driven into a boiling sea. The image was nourished into almost certain reality by the smell of ozone gathering in the air in spite of the sky being completely clear by that time.

I shook the hallucination off, but disquiet remained. There was no fighting it when these moments happened and I surrendered to the inevitable. A storm was coming. Possibly something else as well and the thought of it made me cold.

Bryson put away his cell and sniffed at the air as he reached for the cardboard box I had tucked under my arm. I hoped that he had begun passing the word while I shopped that people should stay off the water. I didn't want to leave the task to young Mrs. Mickle alone, formidable gossip though she was.

We took the direct route to the docks. It came as a bit of a shock to see people cavorting about in costumes in front of the Emporium. There were pilgrims and pirates, women in hoopskirts and bonnets that might have come off an old-fashioned Easter card, soldiers in red coats and soldiers in other color coats with coonskin caps carrying around very realistic muskets, all of which had likely been dragged out of people's attics. There were some bows and quivers of arrows being toted by people in anachronistic dress. There were a lot of whiskers, beards, mustaches, and muttonchops, but these did not come from the attic. They were standard face-wear among certain islanders, though usually they did not gather all their beards in one place. The scene was absent any vendors selling ice cream or popcorn, but the street was as crowded and disorganized as opening day at the county fair and had the same air of expectation.

The sight was more disconcerting that amusing. I was used to everyone in their proper place in proper dress. This trying on of other identities made the world seem skewed at a time when I wanted things to be normal.

Could they truly be oblivious to the danger drawing in around us?

The buildings seemed to know we were threatened. They huddled together as though wishing they could touch. I followed the boards of the Emporium all the way to the peak and the thick hoisting beam that stuck out like a gallows. It was black against the sky.

The public address system had been hooked up, or perhaps was in process because I am pretty sure that grumblings about *quahoggers being plumb brainless* were not part of any official speech though it probably pleased Reverend Ezekiel Burke, a transplant from Salem who was mostly made of cartilage and ill will and the sourest creature our islands had ever been encumbered with.

"They'll need to fumigate if he stays long," I muttered. "Can't someone pass an ordinance?"

The reverend was retired, which was a good thing because there was a lack of takers for his kind of religion and it was generally felt that his attendance was enough to disfigure any event. In part it was his charmless personality but it did not help his cause that he looked like someone had skinned a nightmare and then pulled it on over his skull. Certainly he looked alarmed and aware of danger. Of course, he always looked this way. I couldn't imagine what kept him in the islands.

I made a point of turning away from him. He doesn't approve of my godless family and we don't often speak. He could disapprove of me from sea to shining sea so long as he kept a civil tongue in his head when we were in public. In front of others I demand respect.

Someone was hanging patriotic bunting on the railing in front of the Emporium and singing "Grand Old Flag" in a monotone so flat that you couldn't get a spatula under it. The Emporium always looks vaguely like a memorial monument, or at least classical. It was built by a ship's carpenter just after the civil war and was the sturdiest building in town. It was also the most impressive and had a nice echo when you stood under the overhang. It was where people forgathered when they had some large public event. Whether the Emporium wanted them or not. Another time and I might have hoisted myself onto a convenient barrel and watched the train wreck.

This was apparently a popular idea because Jonas and Saul, local brewmasters, did just that, making sure there was room in the shade for Amos, the Great Dane. As usual, the dog looked despondent. They must be out of beer again. Jonas, the jelly-bellied one, pulled out his portable checkers game and began to set up on the railing. The skeletal Saul, looking more than ever like he had been picked over by crows, turned to survey the colorful and strange spectacle with a slightly malicious eye.

"What on earth are they...?"

"Rehearsal for the Goose Haven Founders Day Pageant," Bryson murmured when I kept gaping and wrinkling my nose at the growing scent of mothballs which was getting thick now that the choir had gotten organized and concentrated their smelly costumes in a large mass about ten feet to our right and downwind.

His words recalled to mind that we were again due for the traditional, seasonal celebration. The news wasn't welcome since I was supposed to give the keynote speech that year. I had a rough draft started a month ago, but it was very rough and I needed something polished by Friday. At the moment, that felt like an impossible goal.

"God is merciless," I muttered. "What, no gallows? No pillory? Where are the typhoid victims? The prohibitionists? I don't think this is historically accurate."

"Don't give them any ideas. We already have one Founders Day casualty," Bryson muttered back. "Mrs. Biggs isn't speaking to Mrs. Warwick. They both want to play the Indian maiden and the committee ruled in favor of Mrs. Warwick since Mrs. Biggs played her last year. Angered at the decision, Mrs. Biggs has taken her spear and moccasins and gone home."

Big cities have short memories, but not so little towns. These champions of good, old-fashioned values forgot them fast enough when it came down to deciding who got to be the princess. Things might be forgiven but they wouldn't be forgotten. This feud could last decades. There was still anger from when the historical society had taken over the local museum from the descendant of the original founder who had turned out to be a scurvy knave who used funds earmarked for acquiring artifacts to repair a leaking roof. This might have been forgiven if the roof had been of period slate, but the old director was a fan of Southwest architecture and had opted for a tile rook imported from Mexico which is, I have to admit, a bit of an eyesore on the gray clapboard building.

"What Indian maiden?" I asked against better judgment. "There was no Indian maiden in Goose Haven. Well, not after the white men came along. Probably not before then either. Nobody lived on the islands back then."

I knew this from doing preliminary research for my speech. And anyway both women were long past the age when they could pass for maiden anything so the quarrel was especially stupid.

Bryson shrugged.

"All I know is the insults are flying and the turbulence has spilled over to the historical society and museum, since each is refusing to work if the other one is there, and it's thrown off everyone's schedules."

And probably no one would be happy with the suggested compromise of having two Indian maidens.

"For pity sakes, let's make a dash for the docks before they see us and demand arbitration," I urged. "I don't want to get dragged into this."

"Now, Tess, you know I don't dash."

But he didn't dawdle either. Bryson knows all about the better part of valor and there were no winners in skirmishes like this one. An onlooker might have thought that I was herding Bryson for his boat, but really it was a question of who was herding whom.

I wondered who else would end up as mortal enemies at the end of the affair. Events like this always spawned quarrels because there were way too many chiefs without any tact, and not enough Indians—and apparently too many Indian maidens—who could abide bossiness in silence.

The reminder of the pageant and the fact that I hadn't chosen a costume had put my other concerns briefly out of mind, but they reappeared the moment we got near the water. It wasn't that I actually felt something bad would happen in daylight, but there was the sense that there was something under the waves. Watching. Aware. Nothing would get me out there after dark.

I was also very aware of the enclosed shed of weathered gray wood. The islands have a lot of historic charm that somehow hasn't carried over to this plain building that has no purpose except to hold the bodies of drowned fisherman until they can be removed. Actually, to hold dead anyone, and that likely included Mrs. Tudor.

Who had died babbling about pirates. That couldn't be good.

Some people will stick their head in the sand and hold it there forever rather than admit to something they don't like or weren't expecting. I am not one of them, but I sure wished I could be. This kind of free-floating fear wasn't dignified in someone who represented the founding family.

"You're being awfully quiet," Bryson said. "This worries me."

"I got some cognac for us," I said as we climbed aboard. It wasn't actually cold, but I felt chilled and took a lap robe out of a locker and spread it over my legs while we cast off. I kept well back from the gunwales and did not peer into the water.

"Good. I could use it. This will be a hard week. Saturday folks will be out decorating in the silent city and I shall have to be on hand to direct traffic and keep the peace. Hopefully the weather will be clear by then or it will be a muddy mess."

"Decorating?" I asked. "Where is Silent City?"

"The cemetery."

The silent city—right. And he meant putting flowers on graves and weeding and straightening tombstones that tend to lean and topple over time. It was a local version of Tomb Sweeping Day, enacted on the anniversary of some triumphal skirmish or other since the weather would be too beastly for housekeeping tasks on the traditional date for funerary maintenance.

Thankfully I was an islander. I didn't need to care about this mainland tradition. Especially since I had real doubts that the body in the mausoleum was actually my great-grandfather.

The Founders Day celebration was another matter. That was an island affair and I would have to find time to work on my speech, since I had stupidly failed to anticipate a cursed treasure washing up on my beach and promised to give it.

The trip was utterly uneventful, discounting a few shrieking gulls who decided to relieve themselves while flapping overhead. Neither bomb hit its target but they drew frowns from both of us when they got too close. Perhaps because Bryson sensed my uneasiness with the advancing hour and my prediction of a storm, he did not really relax either and it was easy to read something into the seagulls' frantic screeching.

We got to the dock to find the boxes of groceries gone. Ben must have come down during the day and collected them. He always did this if I didn't beat him down to the ferry. In some ways, Ben is very old fashioned and it is amusing as well as flattering that he persists in seeing me as a delicate female who can't lift anything heavier than a purse.

Things were eerily quiet as we walked up the path and Bryson commented on the strange seaweed that smelled so awful. It was much more dissolved and disgusting than it had been that morning.

It was nice to have Bryson with me while I gathered up Barney from Ben's place. Ben was either still sleeping or so involved in research that he didn't answer my call. I knew he frequently left his front door open for air and so didn't feel alarmed to find it that way, but the emptiness of his cottage felt strange. Usually there was some sign of habitation.

We went up to the house where my carton of groceries waited on the stoop. I opened the door slowly. Kelvin sat in the middle of the foyer looking at me with large eyes that were probably saying something though I couldn't guess what. He looked away only long enough for a quick nose rub with my unusually subdued puppy.

Shaken and ill at ease, I poured out the cognac and suggested we be comfortable in the parlor, since the groceries could easily wait to be unpacked, but after a single drink Bryson admitted that he needed to be away and I was actually glad to be alone with my thoughts. I was turning into a recluse just like my great-grandfather.

47

The groceries were put up quickly and then I was left with nothing to do except work on my speech or look at boxes of documents, tasks which needed doing but for which I had little enthusiasm.

Kelvin indicated by the patting of my ankle with mostly sheathed claws that he had been locked up indoors all morning and that he wanted to go out back and survey his domain, and since he went out, Barney also followed though hesitantly.

Kelvin took care of some important cat business and Barney followed suit. It was convenient, if a little weird, to have a dog that buried his own messes.

The quiet persisted. There was a wind but it was silent and even the waves' crashes were muted.

I noticed that the ground to my left seemed to be heaving and went to investigate. I wasn't happy to find ants on the move out by the sunflowers. To begin with, one shouldn't have ants on an island. But it was also annoying because the dispossessed could easily decide to take up residence in the kitchen while they were searching out new digs. And they were leaving their old home for good—larvae, leaf mold, a giant I assumed was the queen, everything was being disgorged from the ground.

But they weren't headed for the house. Intrigued at the exodus and wondering where they thought they were going, I followed them along the north wall of the garden where they stayed about twelve inches from the foundation and then up toward the hedge that ringed the cliff that housed the entrance to the smugglers' cave. They passed between boulders I was obliged to scramble over or around, and I was necessarily slow since the rocks were not cemented in and it was a long fall if something gave way.

Once over the rise and through the vines I forgot the ants, my attention being wholly taken up with the horde of seagulls massing on the tiny strip of steep, crumbling land at the top of the cliff. They huddled together on the high ground, terrified into silence but unwilling to take flight. There were also rodents and smaller birds bunching among them. It was as though they had been driven to the cliff's edge and could go no further without falling into the sea.

My flesh began to creep. This was unequivocally abnormal.

48

Lightning crackled to the east and the sun began to plunge westward in a sudden hurry to leave the darkening sky. I looked at my watch. It was later than I had imagined.

"Come on, guys," I said to Kelvin and Barney. "Let's get some dinner and then we'll have treats."

I hoped the birds and animals would be alright out on the ledge during the storm but wasn't sure what to do for them except leave the porch door open. They were welcome to shelter there among the deck chairs and creepers, which grew thick as curtains, if they were brave enough to attempt it. The living drapery would keep out much of the wind and rain.

And ghosts?

I stopped, shaken by the thought. I had been worrying about a nonspecific menace. Some aura of ill will that made it rain. But was this chest attached to a specific entity? And if so, whom? Was it Halfbeard? Or whoever—whatever—had sunk his ship?

Chapter 5

I saw nothing of distinctness there at the margyns, but the form seemed lythe and it glistened green and the eyes peered with malevolent intelligence of one whose rage had clotted and grown hard wyth scars. I saw only one, but unless they be chasing the Calmare then there must be more of them abyding in the deep.
—from the unbound journal of *Halfbeard*

Sunset was a gray-green malevolence and I shut the drapes upon it and made sure that flashlights were on hand. Just in case. Though not really cold enough to justify it, I also had a fire in the library while I sorted through more of the boxes of papers. Love letters, tax records, household hints. The papers and parchments and ink had outlasted their makers and I didn't know if this was wonderful or a horrible comment on our mortality.

It wasn't of the right period but I found a fascinating letter from the thirties about an outbreak of hoof and mouth diseases somewhere in Vermont. Apparently everyone leaving the infected area had to pass through a police checkpoint where they were made to get out of the cars and walk through a trough of disinfectant while their car was washed by a team of men who scrubbed down the tires with some kind of carbolic acid. The disinfectant made leather bleed and quite ruined the ladies' delicate heels and bleached the hem of the indignant gentlemen's woolen trousers.

Though protected by the house I heard the heavens when they parted and upended their flood upon the island. I did not peep through the drapery at the rage outside, but knew that the water would be lashed into a white frenzy by the wind and rain. I prayed that no one from the island was on the sea that night.

Kelvin and Barney stayed close, my poor dog cowering under the onslaught and shivering as I rubbed him with my spare hand.

Though I worked diligently at sorting papers, some limp with freckles of mildew and some so crisp they would break if folded, the loneliness of the island began to intrude on my reading and the awful feeling grew that it wasn't just the storm that was unnatural but that something malignant and wishing to do harm was hiding in it. Enraged, single-minded, coming closer.

I stopped trying to sort papers and gave both hands to the task of rubbing the dog as I listened, sure that at some level I heard strange rustling and tapping just outside the house. The fire grew dull as I watched and waited, as though slowly deprived of oxygen and guttering like a candle. The electricity remained on but it, too, seemed more feeble and I began to feel a bit dizzy and started yawning, though I was too nervous to be sleepy. Perhaps this was some atmospheric anomaly that accompanied the storm.

Reaching a level of discomfort that bordered on fear and possibly hysteria, I decided to try my phone. Ben was the logical choice since he was nearest and my relief when he finally answered was profound. It wasn't a good connection though and I didn't try to prolong the conversation when he began to yawn between the pops and hisses.

Obviously Ben was not spooked—just unusually tired for a night owl. So, probably, I was imagining the feeling that I wasn't alone. Maybe it was time to stop the foolishness and go to bed. Everything would be normal in the morning.

I couldn't resist a last look through the drapes though before retiring. At first it was all just dark, the atmosphere so thick it was palpable, but eventually I could make out lights at Ben's and Mary's cottages. They were distant sparks, but comforting.

Of the sea I could see nothing except, maybe, a faint gray-green light that seemed to bubble up out of the water. The lighthouse was surely working in those dark hours, but the gloom was too thick for me to see or hear it.

Suddenly lines from Poe's "The Raven" came into my head.

Once upon a midnight dreary, while I pondered weak and weary,
Over many a quaint and curious volume of forgotten lore,
While I nodded, nearly napping, suddenly there came a tapping,
As of someone gently rapping, rapping at my chamber door.

I glanced at my door, feeling dread even as I yawned again. It was locked. And all the other doors were locked too. I had checked and double-checked. The storm could knock all night but it would be in vain. I was letting nothing in.

And then rationality came to my rescue. The reason that I was probably feeling like I wasn't alone in the house was because I had company. But it wasn't evil spirits or monsters or whatever I had been imagining coming toward the house out of the darkness.

It was probably the birds and other creatures, sheltering on the back porch. I had propped the door open with a deck chair. That's all I was hearing and feeling—birds and mice and other refugees from the storm settling for the night.

Relieved, I crawled into bed.

* * *

The sunrise had been plagiarized from a Hollywood romantic movie script. The sky was a mix of golden flowers and the flush of a newly wedded bride as the groom pushed aside her wisps of veil. The blue of the sea as it fell under the rising sun was a color so pure and astonishing that sapphires would weep.

But lower the eyes a bit more and you would think you were looking at a disaster film.

Beside me Barney whined and wrinkled his nose.

The animals had indeed sheltered on the back porch and, perhaps frightened by the intensity of the storm, had decided to use it as an outhouse rather than risk the rain.

Beyond, the plants in the yard were laid low, flattened as surely as if an army had marched over them. I would go ahead and cut the sunflowers. They were too broken to save. I would also have to shovel more of that strange seaweed away. It was rank when it started disintegrating in the sun.

A few seagulls remained, the last of the crashers to leave the party. They were so nonchalant in their actions that I didn't bother to worry that they were grounded by broken wings or other injuries. They had simply stayed to point and laugh at my dismay when I saw the yard.

"Ungrateful beasts," I muttered and went to fill a bucket with hot water and to fetch the mop.

With the morning had come a return of the normal, and though I felt pressure to do something about the weirdness around the island, to discover some answers for the strange events overtaking me, the need to clean up the back porch was overwhelming. The smell frightened and maddened me. I also tend to get a lot of thinking done when I am doing housework. And I needed to think about my Founders Day speech.

Ben arrived, with donuts, while I was throwing a last bucket of bleach and water over the planks of the porch.

"Phew," he said. "Isn't it a little late for spring cleaning?"

"Last night a bunch of seagulls took shelter from the storm. On the porch. And had a poop festival. And that damned seaweed smells like the public dump."

"That it does. Never seen the stuff before." Ben grinned and knelt to pet Barney. He was in a really good mood and I hated to spoil it, but last night had forced me to make a decision. "I was so tired that I absolutely passed out last night. The storm didn't bother me a bit."

This was strange. I also had been very tired, but the storm had kept me awake most of the night, a cacophony of noise that intruded on my dreams.

"So, what news from the mainland?" I asked, changing the subject.

"The radiocarbon dating came back. The box is the right age and the gold is from the right place. Everything looks real." Then his brows drew together. "Except the monkey bones—and they *are* monkey hand bones. Spider monkey from Mexico—*Ateles geoffroyi vellerosus*. Those are more recent. Only about ten years old."

I blinked.

"But how…?"

"Damned if I know. But everything else is exactly what it should be. My friend would like to bring in someone from the Smithsonian to verify his tests."

"No." I said this before my brain could catch up with the impulsive refusal.

53

"What?" Ben looked blank.

"No, no one else touches the box. The more people who know about this, the more danger there is—of treasure hunters and other crazies coming to the island to look for artifacts." This was only part of the reason. A very small part.

"But ..." Ben stopped to think about this. "I'm sure that they would be discrete."

"No. Someone would want to get famous, do a TV show or get in National Geographic. This is a big deal, as you say. We can't risk it."

"But it will need to be authenticated before it can be sold or even donated—"

"I'm not selling it."

Those words stunned him into temporary silence.

"But...."

"No. The box and its treasures are not for sale. I may loan them to a museum down the line, but they will not be sold." I had a feeling that the part about loaning the treasure to a museum was a lie, but I had to give Ben something. I knew he was dreaming of a traveling museum show to coincide with the release of his book.

"Okay. Terry can probably handle everything for now. He's going to be disappointed though."

I sighed, hating what I was going to have to do.

"He can have it one more day but then it needs to come back."

Ben began to look annoyed.

"This isn't up for negotiation," I said flatly, hating that I had to make him angry. "I will find the family records of Nicholas Wendover, if they exist. You will have the proof for your book. But the chest comes back to the island. Tomorrow."

I could see the struggle, but he kept his temper and didn't argue.

"Okay. I'll bring it back tomorrow."

"During the day, Ben. Don't go out on the water at night. I'm dead serious about this."

The anger left him and he stared at me. Ben isn't a believer like Harris, but he has been around me and the islanders long enough to know that there is something strange going on in the islands and it mostly centers around Wendover House and its occupants.

"More storms?"

"Yes. Worse ones, I'm afraid. So be careful."

He nodded but didn't ask me how I knew about the weather. That was good because I didn't like talking about premonitions and intuition and stuff like that. Bryson and Harris would be able to accept my gut feeling without feeling creeped out or skeptical about the prediction. Ben probably would not.

Chapter 6

We had then been a score of days in the storm with no discovering of the sun though we journyed ever northward. Then came the call from the bo'sun. There was an island and a break in the awful tempest.
—from the unbound journal of *Halfbeard*

Though Ben probably felt that his research took precedence, my speech for Founders Day was weighing heavily on me and I decided to review my notes and see if they were as thin as I thought they were. It was more important that the speech be tactful than truthful, though managing both would be nice since I hate lying.

Of course, they were thinner than I had feared. It was only the outline of a ghost of an idea without a single crescendo or highpoint even imagined.

I sat at the desk and tried to picture Goose Haven, to pick out its landmarks, hoping it would lend me inspiration. The islands are a little short on typical places of interest since it had never boomed into a tourist attraction. There is Wendover House, a lighthouse—which is Canadian—and a smugglers' cave that everyone pretends doesn't exist.

There is also the Emporium. I called it to mind and studied it from all angles, but it was about as inspiring as raisinless oatmeal until I came to that gallows-like beam at the top of the building. That wasn't anything I wanted to talk about.

However, the street in front of the Emporium was another matter. It was cobbled and old enough to be worn flat in places. It had never been paved over on account of its historic value and it showed the wear and tear of the ages, a physical reminder of how many people have lived there and put it to use.

The stones have been dilapidated mainly by the passage of islanders' feet since there are few vehicles on the island even today. And that dilapidated street was my way in, all those people who had worn the cobbles smooth as they went about their lives. It helped that I had been reading their letters and journals and felt that, at least to some degree, I knew them, or at least what they hoped for, desired, and feared.

I leaned toward the computer and began to type, scavenging images and words of the imagined past.

We have the pleasure today of standing on old ground, in the sunlight with the family and friends who are the children of those who were our parents' family and friends. And as we look out at the sea that nurtures and protects us, we know who we are. The painful search for identity, for roots and belonging which most people face, is spared us. We know who we are and where we belong.

Today we honor those first brave souls who stepped into this wilderness and dared to imagine a civilization here. They defended their dream, rode out every storm, endured the disease and tyranny and war that afflicted those first courageous settlers who dared to put lasting footprints in the sand of our islands.

The phone rang and since I was ready for an interruption I answered.

"Tess," Bryson replied to my hello. "Would you be free for dinner after the Founders Day celebration?"

This sounded social and not ... business related.

My speech was at eleven. I couldn't see celebrating on Goose Haven until dinnertime, even if I thought it would be safe to travel by water after dark.

"Unless you're on duty, could we make it for lunch?"

"Another storm Friday night?" Like I said, Bryson gets it.

"Maybe. It's at least possible. Ben is going to bring the box back tomorrow and I need to work out how to...." I paused.

"To return it?"

"Yes. I don't think UPS is the answer for this job."

"Have you come up with a plan?"

"I'm working on it," I said, looking at the stacks of papers that still needed sorting and reading.

Bryson didn't make any suggestions about how to return the box and I didn't ask for ideas. I had given up asking anyone, except Kelvin, what was going on, or why my great-grandfather had thought or done the things that he did. I still speculated to myself but had accepted the fact that I still didn't know everything that had gone on at Wendover House and that my great-grandfather may not have known either. I would just take it on faith that he had good and sufficient reason for every seemingly crazy thing he did. Like giving back a fortune in possibly cursed pirate treasure.

"Okay. Will you take the ferry on Friday? Or ride over with Ben?"

I hadn't thought about how to get to Goose Haven or that Ben might very well be attending.

"I'll manage something. My speech is at eleven so the ferry would get me there in time."

"Then I'll see you after your speech."

"Looking forward to it. Bye." I hung up the phone and then looked over at my cat. "Okay, Kelvin, if you have some ideas about this mess, now would be a good time to share them with me."

And, as so often happens, the cat answered by jumping into a half-empty box.

"This box?" I asked as he stared at me. "Okay. Do you want to move so I can look?"

He gave me a look of sorrowful contempt. Circled once and lay down.

"So it's in this other box?" I tried. This one was more like three-quarters full.

Kelvin didn't answer. Sighing, I sat down on the carpet and lifted a pile of papers into my lap. And found what I was looking for almost immediately. The papers—the parchment actually— were a lot older and the handwriting was still bold enough to read though the ink was fading.

Not for the first time, I wished that my great-grandfather was available for questions. But he was either dead or else whooping it up in the Land of Midnight Fun and unlikely to reappear in the islands.

I had been looking for a ship's log or perhaps a journal or even letters, not loose papers thrust to the back of an old box filled with household ledgers. But of course the official log had stayed with the ship and perhaps Nicholas Wendover's need to set his adventures down on paper had not allowed for the time needed to send away for a bound book to write in.

As I had noticed before, none of my ancestors had mastered the art of legible writing and the parchment had seen some damage, but I did my best with the villainous cursive and disordered pages.

The islands are fyne and the wynds mostly fair. It's the sea that affrights me now. Too many unnatural shadders (shadows?) *movin in the deep around three bells especially in the First Watch. It's hellish and some say tis ghostesses. Some say tis somping* (something?) *else. Haint or beast, I've seen it scuttling ovr the rocks. If it be the ghost of any man then God help hym. Tis well I sent the Calmare away. I'll not be goin to sea agin.*

My skin tightened. This was it. It had to be. I skimmed until a word caught my eye. I backed up and read more slowly.

It was a dark day we took aboard that crate from the Concepcion. I'd only a few coyns left of my share, but what remained went into the box along with that cursed bundle of bones and I threw it back into the sea. Let the shadders have it. Or the bane my wife speaks of, I prayed. Just take it from me. There had already been two deaths in the islands and the moon was not yet full.

There it was, the *Concepcion*. Confirmation that Nicholas Wendover really was Halfbeard. Ben would be pleased.

I gave up trying to put the pages in order, just began pulling the pieces of yellowed parchment out of the accumulation of other papers. It was unpleasantly suggestive to find rusty stains and spatters, and that his papers had a lot of water damage. In fact, many of them looked like they had been submerged in water and were no longer readable. Had this happened in his time? Or Kelvin's? Maybe Ben's museum friend would know how to rescue the writing.

But the cask did not stay long in the sea. On the nyneth night of September, one year to the day that we took the cargo from the Concepcion, I was roused from sleep by lyghtning. The nyght was full of blow that sounded like damned souls wayling from Hell. Leaving my wife abed, sunk in unnatral deep slumber, I went to the west window where there was a strange lyght rysing from the beach. I knew what it was though I'd never seen a wyllowysp.

The fire was all but out, but I kindled a light. Taking a lantern, I went out in the storm. I was affrighted but would not play the coward. Slow I went, and as I walked the lyght died. All that was left on the beach was the damned casket I had cast away, sitting there open, still filled with pieces of hayte.

That seemed to be it. Frustrated and wanting to be sure that I hadn't overlooked something because the papers were simply out of order, I went back to the beginning and started reading again. It was not an easy task because the entries weren't all dated and the ones that were not damaged by water were yellowed and curling pages that had no numbers.

A lot of the sheets were unreadable and not all of the entries were relevant to my problem, but I set anything from Nicholas aside for Ben and made a stab at putting them in order. Though his words frightened me, there was a fascination in looking at the confession written in his own hand.

I drank myself mad and grew reckless with my lyfe. How else can I explain my deeds, the memory of which I tried so hard to flee? Fear and tyme subdued my more savage nature. The forgetting of my inhuman wyckedness and lust which overran my fear of God or the laws of man was gradual, but after a piece with my gentle wyfe at my side. The dreams ceased and I no longer heard the nytly (nightly?) *lamentations of the plaguey Spaniards sewn up dead and lyve together in the winding sheet and cast overboard to drown.*

"Good God." Barney, young but understanding his job, rushed over to comfort me.

60

So this was what had happened to the crew. Reading the words made me cold and dizzy. How could anyone do that? What sort of monster had Nicholas been? How could I have come from his genes?

We could tell day from nyght but made no discovery concerning the sun. We traveled along the coast seeking an opening in the clouds whereby we could pass through, but no eye could penetrate the gray darkness.

The shadders, they followed us and of a sudden we had become the prey. I do not know what they are that bryng the eerie storm but fear they are the dead, unable to rest because they did not deliver the wytch's cargo and they are here to reproach me.

Reproach him? How about rip his guts out for being the murdering son of a bitch that he was? I found one more entry on a scrap of torn parchment, but where it came in the narrative I could only guess. Possibly before he first cast back the box, though perhaps after when the sea returned it again.

My wyfe asserts that the necklace is gone, that it has been lost. I have told her of the danger we face but she says agin and agin that the necklace was taken. After close questioning, we have set the servants to search for it, a great collar of a thing made from black pearls and a gold coyn, but it has not been found. I fear the shadders may grow bolder and come on land. My wyfe will not suffer. She is protected by her infernal bane. But wyll they take me when the moon bloats full?

Was this why the chest came back? Was still coming back? Because he or his wife had not returned everything he had stolen? And had the shadows taken him? Was that what the wife wanted? Had she discovered that she was married to a murderer and wished him dead?

I couldn't recall from my reading if Nicholas had been another Wendover "lost at sea." Or if he had managed to dodge his deserved fate and die in bed.

Ben would know.

Ben.

"Damn."

My neighbor had twenty-twenty vision but only on his area of focus, which in this case was his book. I didn't think that he would be able to take the long view. For him—for anyone else—this was a kind of spectator sport. I and I alone, as Nicholas's descendent, could theoretically pay off his debt and make this nightmare go away. But it would mean doing something that Ben and the historians would hate. I was feeling discouraged and exhausted. It was not just the weariness of the body but that of an overworked mind and revolted soul. I had had to make too many accommodations with radically new ideas of how the world worked and had to accept improbable and horrible realities.

But then I looked over at Barney snoring as Kelvin bathed him and I began to feel better, or at least stronger. We had weathered all kinds of weirdness. I would figure out what to do this time.

I got up and began to pace. Barney and Kelvin opened their eyes and watched me. I thought about the necklace which was probably worth far more than the coins. It would be beautiful and have a rich history. It was literally a treasure as calculated both by dollars and by history.

Too bad it was also potentially something more.

I reached the bottom of my coffee cup and found my decision there. Really, I had always known what I would have to do. Or at least what I would have to attempt to do.

"Ben will hate me," I said to the cat. "Even if he doesn't know about the necklace."

Barney knew Ben's name and thumped his stumpy tail hopefully.

"But I don't think I have a choice, do I? Maybe it just wants the coin in the necklace, but I can't take that chance. Of course, I've got to find that damned necklace first, gather up everything, the gold and the bones, and dump it back in the sea."

Kelvin raised his head, prepared to listen now that I was getting down to business.

"Then I can let Ben read these notes. They should be enough to finish his book, right? And we have the pictures of the chest if he wants them. I can even photograph the necklace, but maybe it would be best if Ben never hears about that. Losing it would break his heart." It would mean holding back those pages of notes where the necklace was mentioned. Because if he thought the necklace was still in the house somewhere he would give me no peace until I let him look for it.

Kelvin chuffed. He was a very sensible cat and I was glad he agreed with me.

"And Harris will understand. If I tell him. No one wants to lose out on money but ... well, he *believes*." Harris also liked me. Of course, I was the last Wendover. He'd like me if I had tentacles.

Barney began to look serious. Harris was kind but not a real dog person and when he visited it often left me in a pensive, non-tennis-ball-throwing mood.

"The first thing I have to do is find that damned necklace."

I looked around the room, again feeling a little overwhelmed. Kelvin got to his feet.

It was time to stop feeling and to start thinking.

Since there was little hope of discovering the necklace if it had left the island, and since Abercrombie's daughter had been disinclined to leave her gilded prison, I decided that it made sense that the necklace was somewhere within reach. Probably within the house since there had been no other buildings on the island back then.

"They shared a bedroom at least some of the time," I said to the cat. "When Nicholas saw the will-o'-the-wisp he said that he was sleeping with his wife. So what room were they in that he could see the beach?" Assuming the box had washed up on the same bit of land. It almost had to be that way. The rest of the island was stony cliffs and fractured rock.

I went back to the notes and read again about the night the cask came back. Nicholas had looked out a west-facing window which faced the beach, in a room with a fireplace. There were three bedrooms that it could have been and one of them was very small and therefore not a likely choice for the lord and lady to be using.

Of course, the wife could have hidden the necklace anywhere in the house. But there was less chance of her being observed by servants or her husband in her own bed chamber.

Barney sighed and dropped his head in my lap. Kelvin climbed into his favorite box, figuring my brain was working slowly enough that he could take a nap.

"Me too, kid. I sure hope I don't have to rip up the floors and walls. How will I explain that? Harris will have a fit if I ruin anything," I explained, petting his soft ears.

Reading through the papers again for clues while I delayed taking the last drastic step, I finally had to admit that I was dragging my feet because I was afraid to have to ask the gossipy carpenter to come out again and repair my excavations. Scolding myself for cowardice and indecision, I finally got up.

It was time that I actually began looking for the room that most likely was Halfbeard's or his wife's chamber. After all, night would come again all too soon.

Kelvin mewed and I looked up from the papers I was stacking on the desk.

"Do you know which room we want?" I shook my head at his affronted stare. "Sorry, of course you do. What was I thinking, trying to solve this problem myself? Well, lead on then."

The cat jumped out of his box and sauntered from the room and I followed obediently. I had given up feeling strange about taking orders from a cat.

Kelvin led me to the bedroom I had been thinking was the most likely candidate. At least we agreed on this.

Feeling certain that what I wanted would be in the wall and not the floor, which had been explored fairly thoroughly while the electrical work was being done and outlets set into the floorboards of the upstairs rooms rather than the walls, I began with taking down paintings and mirrors. If that wasn't enough then I would start moving furniture away from the walls, but hoped that wouldn't be necessary since it would involve using bar soap on the floors to help the heavy pieces slide without damaging the floor.

I found a suspiciously square bit of lighter plaster behind a painting in the corner of the north wall beneath a painting of a ship. Was it unintentional irony that the painting might well be of the *Calmare*? I hadn't noticed the painting before because there are a lot of pictures in the house and most of them were painted by people with no discernible artistic talent. I squinted at the

64

signature. Maybe I was imagining things, but the writing looked a bit like Nicholas Wendover's spiky hand. And damned if, in the very corner, so tiny as to be a smudge, there wasn't an Indian maiden on what might well be an unpopulated Goose Haven Island.

Putting the painting aside, I looked at the wall. It could be the remains of an old mend to an accident, but I didn't think so. It was about the perfect size for a jewelry box.

"This is it, isn't it, Kelvin?"

He chuffed.

A careful homeowner and respecter of historical properties would call in an expert to look at things before doing anything impulsive to the three-hundred-year-old plaster.

But an expert would have questions about the things I might find. Certainly they would talk about the necklace. And it would take time to get one out to the island. So, I went to get a saw and hammer. I didn't have a stud finder but I didn't need one to get through lathe and plaster, especially not when the site was all but marked with an X.

The first part of the demolition went well. I ended up having to enlarge my first hole when I found the small leather pouch that had been nailed to a stud. The spike affixing it had been driven in deeply and I could not remove it by hand and the leather refused to tear. That meant enlarging the hole so that I could get the hammer inside and remove the spike.

Pulling and pushing and smacking, the dried leather gave way, and though I was able to snag the necklace before it fell—a lovely thing of black pearls with an empty medallion frame that might have held a coin, just as Halfbeard had noted—something else in the bag fell down between the studs. Something heavy and metallic.

I used a word that Barney was too young to hear though I think it amused Kelvin.

I set the necklace and its pouch, which turned out to be a man's glove, on the small table that held the hurricane lamp.

"Now what?" If I pulled the lathe and plaster off all the way to the floor, the painting wouldn't be able to cover the damage.

"Screw it. I'll shove the armoire over here if I have to."

I tried to be careful, I did. But the saw was dull and it was getting dark, so I finally just used the hammer. I stopped every couple of inches to check that there wasn't anything else hiding in the wall, but it remained empty. The whole time I was muttering to Kelvin that this had better be something important and not just a loose nail.

At last, about a foot from the floor, I stopped bashing in the wall. I could reach whatever had fallen. All I had to do was stick my hand in the dark hole and get it.

And I really didn't want to. I told myself I was afraid of spiders. Which was silly. There hadn't been any live spiders in the wall for centuries. What I was really afraid of was touching what might be one of the cursed coins.

"Fine," I said, getting to my feet. My legs and shoes were covered in bits of broken plaster. "Salad tongs will work."

Down to the kitchen we went, Barney and I. Kelvin wasn't interested in a snack, but Barney is always hopeful. I gave him a cookie from the old crock and then fished through my drawers until I had the salad tongs.

It wasn't easy since the hole was too small for my head and I had to work by feel, but eventually I managed to pinch the rogue object in the pincers and pulled up the thing I least wanted to see— another golden piece of hate. This one rather dusty.

It wasn't all that remarkable, but still quite apt, that there should be a blaze of light followed almost immediately by the crack of thunder.

"Enough with the drama," I muttered, feeling both annoyed and also a little fearful at the omen. The necklace and coin I returned to the torn leather bag which was badly desiccated but which managed to hide both items from my sight. I left them on the floor and we all left the room, closing the door behind us though the temptation was to hurl them over the cliff and into the sea.

I lectured myself as I went downstairs to make some tea and to check that the doors truly were locked. Ben would bring the box back tomorrow; I would pack up everything and give it back to the sea in one neat package. Friday was the full moon, if that really mattered, and then life would go back to normal and we would all be fine.

I refused to entertain any other ideas.

Chapter 7

I only just recognyzed the Calmare, she was bloated with tessellations, barnacle strewn and festooned wyth seawrack, her sayls slimed and tattered to the extent of being useless unless drivyn by the devyl's wynd. I wished that I could lay blame for the vysion on inebriety but had tasted no wyne that nyght. I knew it was the damned coyns that called it forth from the deep. They recalled their fell purpose and wished to be reunited so they might fulfill their maker's evil intentions.

—from the unbound journal of *Halfbeard*

Feeling caught in the morass of island weirdness and tired of waiting for Ben to arrive, I decided to drop Jack an email and just casually mention the box washing up on the beach.

I should have known that Jack would immediately assume the worst and demand details of the box, the storm, and what I thought it meant.

Jack, at various times, had thought of us as having a past but also a someday-to-be-again romantic alliance. This was nice, but at present we have a long-distance friendship with some vague assumptions of obligation. How much explanation was he owed?

With Kelvin on the desk advising me, I was deciding just what to tell Jack about the box when there came a knock at the door.

It was rather early for Ben to have returned from the mainland, but I jumped up quickly to answer the summons. However, it wasn't my fellow scribbler on the doorstep, it was Harris Ladd, looking serious. Of course, he always looks serious. It is his natural expression, even if he had attempted to dress down by wearing the gray wool cardigan he sometimes dons when away from the office.

"May I come in?" he asked tentatively when I stood there gaping instead of offering tea and shelter.

"Of course. Sorry, I was expecting Ben. He is bringing the box back today. I wanted it back before the full moon."

"That's good," Harris said gravely, stepping over the threshold and hanging his hat on the coatrack. He didn't greet either dog or cat. Harris isn't a dog person and Kelvin makes him nervous. I think he believes that Kelvin was my great-grandfather's familiar. And he could be right. "Have you thought about how to…."

"Give it back? Not really, but I think it may actually work this time. I, ah, found something in Nicholas Wendover's bedroom. Part of the treasure that was missing."

"Really?" Harris began to look animated.

"Yes, you can look if you want. I just wouldn't touch anything. It feels…."

"Contaminated?" He grimaced.

"Yes. That's exactly what it feels like." I brushed at my skirt, almost certain I could feel something slimy on my hands, though I had never actually touched any of the cursed coins. "Look, I had to knock a hole in the wall to get it out. We'll need to have someone in to repair it. Sorry."

Harris didn't sigh but I knew he wanted to. Any damage to Wendover House might as well be damage to him.

"I suppose retrieving the dread object was more important than the plaster," Harris said bravely. He really talks like that.

"I think so." We started up the stairs. "Not that I'm not happy to see you, but why have you come?"

"Well, it's not truly important. Just some gawmy gossip, but Bryson and I discussed it and I thought I had best tell you that we've had a death in the islands and there is bound to be some talk since the deceased has family."

"Someone besides Mrs. Tudor died?"

"Yes, a mainlander. He did not heed the weather bulletin and went out last night. There was an accident and he drowned. He came for the celebration."

I stopped outside the bedroom door, feeling a little ill. I hadn't thought about the tourists who would be here for the Founders Day Pageant.

"And?" This news by itself was not enough to bring Harris to the island.

"And the night before, whilst inebriated, he claimed to have seen a ship—a fire ship. Which in some cultures betokens that there is a treasure hidden nearby."

"It also betokens death in every damned case I've ever heard of. It's like a nautical banshee."

"Yes. But he was drunk and overcome by the idea of treasure, and chose to chase the ship as one would a rainbow...."

"And the storm killed him for it."

Harris hesitated. He prefers to be precise and he feared it wasn't actually the storm that had killed the man. I'll grant the distinction of being killed by a storm and what was hiding in it, but not in matters of public relations.

Some people are indefatigable in their efforts to do stupid things for money. My surge of anger was partly about feeling some sense of responsibility because it seemed that this curse was caused by a family member. But it was also plain old anger that this stupid, greedy stranger could cause more problems for us.

Some of the mainland coastal towns are within the outskirts of the bane's influence. The people are grateful that their fishing remains good while other regions are in trouble. Mostly they don't ask questions about what happens in the islands because the story of the Wendover bane is still vaguely remembered in fishing families. But those further inland do not benefit directly from the islands' good fortune and they do ask questions which sometimes find their way into the press whose denizens are always hungry for sensational stories. There is a saying in the news business: if it bleeds, it leads.

"It wouldn't matter so much, if Mrs. Tudor had not had her vision of a pirate vessel as well. People have long memories and aren't always careful about where they reminisce about past visitations," he finally said. "There's been some talk among the visitors."

"Harris, I don't know what to say, except that I hope everyone is paying attention to the weather bulletins from Bryson and staying off the water at night. I'm doing what I can to fix this, but I keep getting sandbagged with problems outside of my skill set. A little warning would be nice."

"Keeping people off the water at night shouldn't be a problem," Harris said, ignoring my implied criticism. "It never was a problem here in the islands. Those on the mainland ... they have mostly forgotten to have fear."

I nodded, letting the matter go, and opened the door to Nicholas's sleeping chamber. We stepped into the bedroom. Harris winced when he saw the wall and the dried wood lathes and plaster on the floor, but his attention went at once to the glove on the rug near the window. In the sunlight it looked a bit like a shriveled hand.

"Use the tongs if you want to see the coin that's inside." I didn't offer to fish it out. "The damned coins are associated with something called monkey leprosy."

Harris actually shuddered.

"That's alright. I feel no need to see the damned things. Your great-grandfather described them well enough."

"You knew about them then?"

"Not that they were specifically cursed, he may not have known that, but that there were two gold coins in the chest, yes."

Not for the first time I felt like shaking Harris for withholding information from me. Again. He would let me do it too. Because I was the last Wendover. This kept me from giving in to the impulse. That and the fact that I knew he acted out of what he thought was kindness and the danger of overwhelming me with peculiar and sometimes even bad news.

"There are three gold coins now. And the necklace. The jewelry may not have anything to do with the problem, but Nicholas thought it might, so I'm sending it back, just in case. I don't want anyone else dying." Especially me.

And I was beginning to wonder if this was a possibility. Ghosts in literature and legend are usually unaware of the people who witness their movements. The white ladies and black monks make their eternal rounds at their appointed places at the predetermined hours, unaffected by human presence. But I know from personal experience that ghosts can be completely aware of the corporeal world and can seek to influence it.

I was beginning to think that whatever was out there was aware of me. At least was aware that I was a Wendover, and as the family's last representative, it wanted something only I could give it.

Harris stared at me for a moment, probably wondering how Nicholas had contacted me with news from beyond the grave, and then his consternation broke. His smile was relieved.

"You found his log? Where was it? I should very much like to read it."

"No log, just some notes. But there is enough there to give me the general outline of the situation."

When Harris made no move toward the yellowed glove, I gestured that we should leave. Just seeing the thing made me nervous and, though it was completely unreasonable, I didn't even want to breathe the air of the room so long as the coin was in it.

"Did you know that Nicholas killed the crew of the ship he stole the treasure from?" I asked Harris. "They were sick with something he called monkey leprosy and he sewed them up—living and dead—into a sail and threw them overboard."

Harris looked distressed and also revolted. He doesn't like staring such brutal unpleasantness in the eye.

"I know every family has black sheep, but this guy was a real winner," I said. "I kind of hope the ghosts, or monsters, or whatever this thing is got him in the end."

"It was said that either he died by accident, or that he killed himself." Harris got out a handkerchief and mopped his brow. "He did not die peacefully in his bed."

"So, chalk one up for the other team. Or maybe three, if they scared Mrs. Tudor to death and lured the drunken treasure hunter out to sea."

Harris hesitated.

"What?"

"There were probably more deaths through the years. It is said that deaths come in threes whenever the box appears and it seems to have come every decade or so. At least during Kelvin's life."

That was a lot of deaths. Thirty every century. Somehow, this had to end. Hopefully returning this last coin would do the trick.

"Ben doesn't know that part of the story," I said. "I'd prefer to keep it that way."

"I agree. There is no way that the family could be held legally liable but the whole thing would attract the sensational press if he were to mention it in one of his books."

72

Leave it to Harris to worry about that aspect of things ahead of anything else.

"I know," I said soothingly. "That's why I wouldn't let Ben's museum friend call in specialists to examine the box and the coins. The matter must be contained."

We reached the foot of the stairs. Since Harris didn't put his hat back on immediately I suggested he stay for lunch. I didn't have much I could prepare on short notice, but he liked baked beans on toast and that I could manage.

As I prepared our meal, augmenting the beans with a tablespoon of marmalade and the remainder of a very old tin of curry powder, Harris read through the papers I had found. He rearranged them slightly, perhaps giving them more coherence, though obviously not improving the grim tale because he cycled through expressions of amazement, fear, and disgust as he read.

"Kelvin didn't tell me about this. If he knew and I am inclined to believe he did. This is simply...."

"Yes." I set our plates on the table. "As I said before, I hope the *whatever the hell it is out there* got him. He deserved it."

Harris tutted at my bloodthirstiness but didn't contradict me.

"It comes from marrying men from *away*," he said fussily. "They almost always have bad blood."

I wondered if he was thinking of Jack.

"Some of the local blood isn't so great either."

That reminded me that I still hadn't answered Jack's email. I would need to do that before he climbed on a plane and flew out to see what kind of trouble I was in. Jack had done that before, bless him.

"So, you plan to return the box on Friday evening?" Harris asked.

"At the full of the moon. Nicholas mentions it as important so...." Kelvin jumped in my lap and fixed me with his unblinking stare. "The full moon is good? You approve?" I asked the cat, forgetting Harris was there and rather nervous about the cat.

Kelvin lay down in my lap and began to wash his paws.

"Yes, Friday night is a go," I said, looking up and finding Harris staring at me with something close to consternation. He can accept everything about the family except that we have always had cats. That look exactly like Kelvin. In fact, I think Harris believes that all the cats *are* Kelvin. "It's okay, Harris. I talk to the cat, but he doesn't talk back. He isn't a demon or anything." Though he wasn't just a cat either. I didn't try to fool myself about that.

Barney sighed and dropped his head onto my feet, no doubt wishing that he, too, could sit in my lap.

"I talk to the dog, too, you know. He doesn't answer either. It's just the habit of someone who lives alone." I broke off some crust and passed it to Barney. I know, I shouldn't feed him from the table, but usually it's just us and Barney really likes toast.

Harris picked up a fork and began eating. I didn't think that I had convinced him of my cat's innocence.

Chapter 8

Never before did I believe that the dead would truly ryse up in judgment if not layd to rest in consecrated ground. But I have seen with myne own eyes, those drowned faces and barnacled bones walking out of the surf. They stay on the shore for now, waiting, demanding I return what is theyrs. Horror dwells upon me day and nyght. I must find some way to do what they want. My wyfe who is wyth child must not be allowed to see them lest it harm the babe resting in her womb.
—from the unbound journal of *Halfbeard*

Ben reappeared that afternoon. There were circles under his eyes which were an unattractive shade of red in whites that looked a little jaundiced.

I had expected him to plead once more for the box to stay with his friend, but after he set it on my counter, he went immediately to wash his hands. I thought that, perhaps once the excitement of discovery had worn off, he was beginning to find the box as repellant as I did and to maybe question the wisdom of possessing it. At least I hoped that was what he was thinking and not plotting how he could convince me to keep it, or to let him have it. All other considerations aside, I didn't think that the box was good for Ben.

Or anyone.

Even if you didn't believe in psychic contagion, the damn thing might somehow still be carrying some corporeal disease.

My offer of tea was accepted and we sat down on the kitchen bench with our cups and some muffins and ate in silence. It wasn't an angry quiet, but one filled with unusual tension. Ben was troubled.

"I don't believe in curses and ghosts," he said at last. "I just don't. It isn't rational."

"Don't be an idiot," I said mildly. "Think about where you live. Everyone here believes in curses and they are all quite sane."

"I don't mean *that*. I'm talking about this box and those coins … it's just a legend that ignorant seamen believed in. Treasures can be cursed, of course, but it doesn't mean the crazy people who mumble their spells over it really have any real power," he insisted but looked uneasily at the box on the counter. It wasn't actually still wet but it gave the impression of being damp and slimy. It wouldn't have surprised me if something squishy and tentacled had come wiggling out of it.

"Have you found any of Halfbeard's papers yet? Does he talk about the box?" Ben asked.

"I've excavated to the right layer, I think, but am still sifting," I lied. I had picked all the papers up and locked them in the desk. I wanted to get a fire box for them. All the papers should be stored more carefully, but I figured rubber totes would do fine for most of them. "I should have something by this weekend. Right now I just want to get through this Founders Day speech."

Ben grunted.

"What a confoundedly stupid time to have a celebration," he complained, though it was actually the perfect time for this sort of thing if one wanted tourist dollars and the islands most emphatically did. That meant getting in your licks between the mainland blueberry and cranberry harvests. "Is your speech ready?"

"Yes. More or less. It just needs a tweak or two. What I need to do is practice it out loud. I hate public speaking."

"Do you want me to read it over? Maybe punch it up a little?"

He didn't mean that to be insulting about my writing abilities. It was a nice offer, an olive branch even. After all, Ben was a great writer. He probably could punch up the speech and make it something for the history books. But that would mean spending more time with him and I didn't want to have to keep lying about stuff, not even by omission.

"That's okay. I need this to sound like me. To sound sincere and homegrown. You know, not too slick. Or good."

Ben grinned briefly and got to his feet. He rubbed at his face. He looked absolutely haggard.

"I need to get home and start writing. I've been away a lot this week and haven't gotten nearly as much done as I had hoped."

I felt guilty. Ben really didn't look well.

"Thanks for everything. I should have something for you on Saturday."

"Good. I need to put this baby to bed. I have other deadlines. By the way, do you want to ride over to Goose Haven with me tomorrow? You could practice your speech on me if you wanted."

"Thanks. That would be great."

Chapter 9

The whyspers came from all around—at sea. From land, above, below. When we heeded them not they turnd to slurs and snarls that seemed to draw ever closer. Those below decks heard them too as well as scratching at the syde of the ship where something threatnyng tried to gain admittance. Even down in the lazarette they heard the snarls and scratching as if giant rats gnawed at the timbers.
—from the unbound journal of *Halfbeard*

The weather was lovely for Founders Day. I wondered if I would get credit for it. Certainly I would have been blamed had it stormed.

Barney knew that something was up when I took the step of putting on makeup and he began to look concerned. He wasn't used to being left alone and it caused me some guilty pangs. I just hoped Kelvin would be a good enough babysitter since Ben was going to be away too.

Going on the theory that an easy walk is not an attractive walk, I was wearing moderate heels and a slightly tight skirt. My neckline dipped a couple of inches into a tasteful V but even the Reverend Burke could not claim it plunged and my arms were covered.

I had decided against wearing a costume. There hadn't been time to dig out something appropriate. It seemed best that I should go as myself and not feel self-conscious when Bryson and I dined later.

A glance at my watch said it was time to go so I propped open the back door, put food in the already empty dishes, and headed for Ben's cottage.

Ben was quiet on the trip over, withdrawn though not angry. That silence was unlike him, but since I had a head full of my own thoughts, I decided not to try and draw him out. Anyway, what was there to say? The box had to go back.

The various groups coagulated into colorful clots along the street and condensed around the stage, mostly sorted by era but sometimes by color, as in the case of the choirs. I have noticed that

there is ecumenical harmony at official functions, probably
because everyone agrees to pursue a separate but equal doctrine.
At least in public. What they feel in their hearts is another matter.
As far as the world of the mainland is concerned, the Catholics
love the Methodists and everyone enjoys pancakes with the
Baptists and snow cones with the Episcopalians.

The stands were full of tourists from both the U.S. and
Canada who were looking for some wholesome entertainment.
They would get it too. I bet the pageant wouldn't have one witch,
execution, pirate, or sea monster in it. There would be no ugly
histories reenacted in the play. They would learn a lot about fishing
and pine trees, and in a punctual manner since the program would
by God start on time.

Mr. Hazeltine, chairman of the Committee for Better Motion
Pictures, took the stage to introduce me. The man is an utter and
extreme bore and isn't particularly well informed about local
history, but it hardly matters. He sounds like Sean Connery and
always gets asked to narrate plays and introduce speakers. The
only holdouts are the Catholics who won't ask him to call Bingo
on account of his being a Methodist.

My speech wasn't long, but I don't think they wanted it to be.
I spoke mainly to Harris and a little to Ben who were both in the
audience, since I don't like public speaking. The words were
sincere and the crowd not critical, either because they knew me, or
because they didn't, so I got a lot of applause and was able to
escape before I got sunburned.

The all-church choir took the stage next and sang "State of
Maine Song," which I had never heard before. After that the choirs
separated by robe color. Red robes sang first. I sat through "What a
Friend We Have in Jesus" and then Bryson appeared at the edge of
the stage. His smile was muted but that meant it was genuine. He
saved the toothy grin for the tourists. I nodded when he jerked his
head toward the chowder house and at the next exchange of choral
groups I snuck away from the stage.

"Nice speech," he said.

"And short."

"That too. But this is an audience that likes brevity."

"That's what I figured."

Mike was in the throes of some kind of proprietor's ecstasy. He had probably made a killing with his wife's fresh donuts and fishcakes and was now hawking bread bowls filled with chowder to the crowded table he waited.

To Bryson's amusement, I ordered grilled cheese and a salad. They are taking bets about when I will learn to like shellfish. They don't know it, but that will be *never*.

"So, tonight's the night?" Bryson asked suddenly. I noticed that he wasn't volunteering to be my right hand any more than Harris had.

"Yes, the moon is full. It seems inadvisable to let this continue indefinitely. What if it drives the fish away?" Or more people died?

He nodded and said nothing else.

I would have preferred the crème brulée for desert but am not inflexible and the chocolate ganache was heavenly. I couldn't stick my spoon in it and not give it full attention which means that whole gluttony is a deadly sin thing slipped my mind for a while. It would have stayed slipped if Reverend Ezekiel Burke hadn't walked in and reminded me.

The reverend was not looking good. Even by candlelight he appeared haggard, like someone had washed his insides in hot water and made his bones shrink. And I recognized the look in his eyes. This was a fanatic who was terrified of something beyond human sin.

"Oh hell," I said and put down my spoon.

Bryson turned his head and took in the black-clad skeleton with wild eyes.

"What's he on about now?"

"I'm betting pirates. Or maybe ghost ships. I better take him outside before he scares the tourists."

"Have you actually seen them?" Bryson asked, surprising me.

"Felt them. Or something." I met his gaze. It was a relief to be with someone who understood, even if that meant that the impossible was once again upon us. "Ben will hate me, but I think I'm going to have to give the box back—treasure and all."

"It won't do any good," Bryson warned. "Not long term. Kelvin tried."

"But I can't keep it. We can't keep having these storms. Someone else will die. And maybe this time it will work. I've found a piece of the missing treasure. Maybe now the collection will be complete and they will finally go away for good."

Bryson was still blinking with surprise when I got up and approached the wild-eyed minister.

"Reverend Burke, let's step outside and get some air. You'll feel better." Sometimes a strong suggestion can be efficacious. But not this time.

"The damned have come! The spawn of hell are—" I grabbed his arm and spun him around so he faced the door. He had lost a lot of weight and I am not a small person. Shock was also on my side. He wasn't used to being manhandled and I had him out of the chowder house before he had attracted too much attention from the visitors. The locals were, of course, watching with interest. But no one was going to interfere. They all agreed that this affair was mine to handle.

"Get a grip," I ordered him, keeping my voice low as I marched him around the side of the building. "I know about the spawn and will be taking care of it tonight."

"Satan must be rebuked! Evil must—"

"Reverend, I've got it covered. You need to stay away from Satan and the spawn and let me deal with it. It isn't safe for you to be out at night."

"God is my shield. He shall protect me when—"

I got right up in his face.

"Stay away from the sea. Stay away from the shore. I mean it. And not another word about any of this in front of the tourists or Bryson will arrest you for a drunk and disorderly."

With that I turned and went back inside. I hoped he saw reason, otherwise Bryson really might have to arrest him for being crazy and disorderly.

Mike gave me a relieved look when I came back in the door alone. I smiled reassuringly and went back to my table.

"I ordered you another ganache, but Mike says lunch is on the house," Bryson said, pushing the fancy dish my way.

"Thanks. This is the kind of day that calls for double dessert." And I ate it. If anything happened, I wanted it reported that the condemned had enjoyed a hearty last meal.

It was only a little after one when we left the chowder house but the horizon was already gathering clouds along the margins. Another storm was coming.

I felt a small trill of nerves. As I had told everyone, it was the full moon and tonight it was the night that I returned the damned box to its even more damned owners.

"Home?" Bryson asked me.

"Yes, please. I have some things I need to do."

I didn't really and was glad when he didn't ask me to elaborate. I had been good and brave all day long. I needed some time to pet my dog and do some private panicking.

Chapter 10

Most tymes a good blade doth put heart in a man, but though we had blades aplenty and many a deck gun and cannons, yet we dyd not feel safe from the evyl that stalked us. And I knew no means by which our eventual fates could be bettered. Every nyght they grew more real to me and I came to wonder if someday they shall have th pow'r to walk through woode and stoene. What are these ab-natral creature?
    —from the unbound journal of *Halfbeard*

Sunset. The clouds moving on the islands were purple, livid with threat and streaks of fire, but the glowing fog soon hid this masterpiece of rage from my view.

I waited for full dark before stepping outside. I did not want to chance being seen and questioned by Mary or Ben.

Part of me expected to find water-logged zombies rotting on the doorstep when I opened the door, but there was nothing there except a few fingers of mist. Something was keeping the clouds away from the house. That was good. I needed to know that I had a safe retreat if I was going to keep my courage. I tried not to think about the strange sea wrack that had moved closer to my door with each passing night.

The fog closed in as soon as I left the narrow perimeter of light around the house. Though stifling and airless it was also extremely cold, almost an ice fog. I had trouble breathing as I inched down the path but suspected the problem was as much psychological and maybe psychic as it was physical. I was very frightened under my robe of calm intention. It wasn't my first ghostly encounter but it was the first time that I felt menaced, that the other meant me harm. *What are these ab-natual creatures?* Halfbeard had asked. Something more than ghosts, surely. But could they become corporeal? It had me belatedly rethinking my assumption that the family bane could—and would—keep me safe.

There was a flashlight in my jacket pocket but I have learned that in dense fog, all it does is light up the upper half of my body and is actually a deterrent to sight while marking me with a spotlight. Also I needed both hands for holding the chest which I had wrapped in my ruined coat. It was going to be left on the beach too. I didn't want it anymore.

I looked back once. The house lights were still on but they were vague and indistinct. The fog was also swallowing sound. That was by design, I was sure. Fog to hide the enemy here and rain everywhere else in the islands to deter witnesses. There were lights in the other two houses, which seemed very far away, but they were swallowed up by the thickening stench and I had a suspicion that in them, my neighbors slumbered in a deep, unnatural sleep.

I could barely hear Barney's braying and Kelvin's howls of warning and indignation. I knew my pets wanted to be with me and would defend me to the death. And that was why I had locked them in the pantry. If there was any dying that night, it would not be done by them.

Up from the beach there crept a hideous bouquet of rot and sea wrack. Since there was no wind I had to infer that the stench was growing because something horrible was getting closer. That was expected but my legs were shaking as the fear grew.

I forced myself down to the beach. The tide was out but I didn't trust the water at all. The usual physical laws did not seem to apply that night. It took all my effort, but I put the box out at the high-tide line about ten feet from the churning water. My limbs simply refused to move me any closer to the surf. I knelt in the wet sand and opened the chest so that whatever was out there in the waves could easily see inside. In the rising light of the green phosphorescence coming up from the sea I could make out the three coins, the necklace, and to one side the shriveled glove that looked like it might well have fit the denuded monkey paw.

Then I climbed on a distant rock to wait. My rational mind kept screaming at me to flee, but somehow I knew that I had to remain as a witness, if this handing over of cursed treasure was to work. I sat on my high rock with my flashlight clutched in my hand, though I knew I wouldn't have the courage to turn it on. I looked and looked into the fog. My eyes have never stared so hard, but the vapor's density defeated me. It was left to my nose and ears to tell me when danger came and when it was gone.

I know that we are all going to die. Of course we are. But there was a big difference between we are all going to die *someday* and I'm going to die *now*. After a while it wasn't courage that kept me on that rock, it was terror. Paralyzing, stop-the-breath horror.

I'm not saying I ever saw Halfbeard's *shadders in the deep*. I finally lost what nerve I had and buried my face in my knees and clapped my hands over my ears in an attempt to keep the stench from choking me and also to spare my eyes if they managed to actually see any of things I heard moving in the mist. But I knew they were there—very close—and when the tide went out and the mist rolled away, the cursed box was gone.

By then my limbs were asleep and I had a terrible pain shooting through my back and neck. But I was alive and alone.

I fell off my rock as I tried to climb down and bruised my knees on the smaller stones. I had to stagger crab-wise back to the house, but I was euphoric and wept with happiness when I opened the pantry door and saw Barney and Kelvin looking up at me with frantic eyes.

Chapter 11

I knew the nyght that the Calmare was lost. It took four days for word to reach the island, but I already kenned what fate had befallen her and my crew. I can but pray that the evyl is avenged now and wyll come no more to the island seeking the last of the treasure.

—from the unbound journal of *Halfbeard*

I went down to the beach the next morning to look for tracks around my rock, but the tide had swept the sand bare, supposing that ghosts actually left footprints. My coat was gone too. That was no great loss since I would never have worn it again.

Evidence of my encounter would have been nice, but it was enough that the chest was gone and that I was alive.

Ben joined me as I stared out at the sea which was beautifully calm and the horizon completely clear of atmospheric blemish.

"No more storms?" he asked.

"Not today anyway." I looked down at him, kneeling in the sand and petting my dog. Ben was a good neighbor. I was sorry that I had had to give his treasure away. "Want some breakfast? I could make blueberry pancakes."

"That would be great. I had barely started my bowl of dinner vegetation when I fell asleep. I guess I got too much sun yesterday," he said, getting to his feet. I noticed that he looked refreshed. Whatever had been ailing him had departed. "How about it, Barn? Want to share some grub?"

Barney barked and wagged his stumpy tail. He always wants to share some grub.

* * *

I stared at the phone as though I wished to be certain that it wasn't telling lies. The news shouldn't have shocked me, but somehow it did. I thought the weirdness with the chest was over.

"Tess?" Bryson's voice was worried.

"I'm here." But I said this to the air.

Reverend Burke was dead? Had the idiot come down to the sea after my warning and tried to rebuke the waters? Should I be horrified? Relieved that he was dead? Of course, it might be that his demise was not related.

"It wasn't a lynching or something normal like a plain old murder that got him?" I asked at last, hardly daring to hope that it could be unrelated.

"It looks to be another accidental drowning. He was tangled in seaweed." Bryson's voice was dry.

Seaweed.

"People are going to start avoiding the Founders Day Festival."

Bryson grunted.

I should have been more upset at the news of the reverend's passing, but I hadn't cared for the man and was glad the dead man wasn't someone I liked.

And, if the legends were true, then his was the third death that came with these visitations and everyone else would be safe.

Until the box came back.

If it came back. Maybe it was gone for good since I had found the third coin.

"Are you going to do DNA tests on this body?" I finally asked, taking a seat at my desk. My slumped posture would have brought reproof from my grandmother.

They hadn't run tests on the last victim and I was actually curious about what such tests would reveal, though I knew it might well open a Pandora's box of outsider questions and official interest if the results came back with some whacky three-hundred-year-old Spanish DNA, but it would be really nice to know what the hell it had been out there in the fog.

"It's a clear case of accidental drowning. The coroner will do an autopsy, of course, but I don't think we need put anyone to the expense of genetic testing."

Yes, he was drowned, but by whom? Reverend Burke wasn't a drunk and he didn't own a boat so there would have been no reason for him to be down by the shore or docks.

Except that he had probably felt the need to confront evil and, this time, evil had been stronger than his indignation and righteous threats.

"I'll let you know how things go, but I don't think there is anything to worry about."

The death was highly suspicious, but I was betting that the new coroner would see it Bryson's way. He was originally from Great Goose and understood how things worked. Bryson and Everett are the law in the islands and what they say is truth is the accepted reality. The old coroner, Samuel Shawley, might have been more troublesome being from *away*, but he had gotten conveniently absentminded and even incompetent. Not that anyone in the islands had complained too loudly about his inefficiency. It mostly suited us, as the post was just something we needed filled to keep outsiders happy. But the old coroner had a wife, just enough younger and slightly less absentminded, who forced her husband to retire before he had an accident on the job. So now we had a new examiner of deaths, Nathan Shipp. Nathan is very aware that Maine is proud of the fact that we have the lowest violent crime rate in the United States.

"Let me know when the funeral is. I'll send flowers."

"Will do. Doubt there will be much of a turnout for this one, so no undue attention."

I suspected he was right.

"How is the silent city today?" I asked. "At least it isn't raining."

"Not as quiet as I'd like given that most of the people are dead," Bryson said. "Everett will have to mind the reverend's paperwork. I need to be off before someone else gets territorial about the tombstones and we have an incident of domestic violence. People—honest to God. They have no respect for the dead."

I wondered if he was aware of the irony in that statement given what we had just been talking about.

"Okay. Well, don't be a stranger," I said and hung up the phone.

Kelvin and Barney were both waiting patiently, eyes fixed on my face. It was clearly time for a snack. I have found that when one is an animal, apparently almost any time is right for a snack. This seemed a sensible attitude to me given they didn't care about weight gain.

"It's going to be a beautiful day," I said. "Shall we have a picnic on the beach? We can drop the pirate's papers off with Ben on the way. He'd like that."

It had taken me a few minutes to remove all papers with references to Nicholas's wife and the necklace. The expurgated account was still pretty sensational and proved his supposition.

Barney barked and wagged his tail. Kelvin stalked away. He didn't care about Ben's book and liked napping a whole lot more than picnics.

"Fine. I'll leave your lunch in the pantry, party pooper."

I swear, he snorted.

Epilogue

I finally found one of great-grandfather's journals along with a few more notes from Nicholas, who sounded ever less sane. This journal was from the late nineties. After reading the first few pages of spider prints, I decided that I was rather glad that I hadn't discovered the thing before my moonlight encounter with Halfbeard's cursed ghosts. Nicholas had been out of his mind with guilt and superstitious dread, which might cause him to imagine things. My great-grandfather didn't come across that way.

Kelvin didn't specify that he was talking about the chest in his entry, but it was pretty obvious what he meant and his words were scary.

The centuries have strengthened the monstrosity, given it power over the weather—even here, at least at night. I don't know what else the damned thing wants, why it sends its pawns ashore. Perhaps it searches. Every ten years it casts its chest upon the beach and at the next full moon I throw it back again with something else added, this time a monkey's paw, a charm which my father purchased from a South American seaman. But nothing pleases it.

I think what it, or maybe they—since I see figures in the unnatural fog—chiefly want is the pirate who killed them and stole the cursed treasure they were bound to by that wizard's blood magic. But it is not within my power to give him to them. If I could do it, I would. The man was a damned villain. It may be that I shall have to dig up his bones and add them to the chest if any actually remain.

"Ugh." I had a feeling he meant it and hoped passionately that this drastic step would never have to be taken. Grave robbing just wasn't in the cards.

But about Halfbeard's character, Kelvin and I agreed. The man had been a damned villain and a murderer.

The cat mewed at me, patting the book with his paw.

"You think I should read more?"

The cat almost shrugged.

"Later then. You want to go outside?"

Barney knows the word *outside* and jumped to his feet and barked happily.

"Okay, come on."

Reading Kelvin's journal would probably be instructive, if laborious, a good way to spend the winter when I huddled near the fire and pretended it wasn't snowing. I didn't think that time was far away. Winter was coming early.

And maybe I would learn more about my family, my grandma. It couldn't be all bad news, could it?

And if it was bad news, well, forewarned is forearmed. At least that's what they say.

About the Author

Melanie Jackson is the author of over 60 novels. If you enjoyed this story, please visit Melanie's author web site at www.melaniejackson.com.

eBooks by Melanie Jackson:

The Chloe Boston Mystery Series:
Moving Violation
The Pumpkin Thief
Death in a Turkey Town
Murder on Parade
Cupid's Revenge
Viva Lost Vegas
Death of a Dumb Bunny
Red, White and a Dog Named Blue
Haunted
The Great Pumpkin Caper
Beast of a Feast
Snow Angel
Lucky Thirteen
The Sham
Murder by the Book

The Butterscotch Jones Mystery Series
Due North
Big Bones
Gone South
Home Fires
Points West
The Wedding
Wild East

The Wendover House Mystery Series
The Secret Staircase
Twelfth Night
On Deadly Tides

Pieces of Hate

Miss Henry Mystery Series
Portrait of a Gossip
Landscape in Scarlet
Requiem at Christmas

Wildside Series
Outsiders
Courier
Still Life

The Book of Dreams Series:
The First Book of Dreams: Metropolis
The Second Book of Dreams: Meridian
The Third Book of Dreams: Destiny

Medicine Trilogy
Bad Medicine
Medicine Man
Knave of Hearts

Club Valhalla
Devil of Bodmin Moor
Devil of the Highlands
Devil in a Red Coat
Halloween
The Curiosity Shoppe (Sequel to A Curious Affair)
Timeless (Sequel to Club Valhalla)
Nevermore: The Last Divine Book